A DANGEROUS FRIENDSHIP

Recent Titles by Jeffrey Ashford from Severn House

THE COST OF INNOCENCE
A DANGEROUS FRIENDSHIP
DEADLY CORRUPTION
EVIDENTIALLY GUILTY
FAIR EXCHANGE IS ROBBERY
AN HONEST BETRAYAL
ILLEGAL GUILT
LOOKING-GLASS JUSTICE
MURDER WILL OUT
A TRUTHFUL INJUSTICE
A WEB OF CIRCUMSTANCES

Writing as Roderic Jeffries

AN AIR OF MURDER
DEFINITELY DECEASED
AN INSTINCTIVE SOLUTION
AN INTRIGUING MURDER
MURDER DELAYED
MURDER NEEDS IMAGINATION
SEEING IS DECEIVING
A SUNNY DISAPPEARANCE

A DANGEROUS
FRIENDSHIP

Jeffrey Ashford

This first world edition published 2008
in Great Britain and the USA by
SEVERN HOUSE PUBLISHERS LTD of
9–15 High Street, Sutton, Surrey, England, SM1 1DF.

British Library Cataloguing in Publication Data

Ashford, Jeffrey, 1926-
  A dangerous friendship
  1. Suspense fiction
  I. Title
  823.9'14[F]

ISBN-13: 978-0-7278-6687-5   (cased)

All Severn House titles are printed on acid-free paper.

Printed and bound in Great Britain by
MPG Books Ltd., Bodmin, Cornwall.

One

Querry Brade, six miles from Trentford, was a late fifteenth-century, half-timbered house; once a monastic inn, it had two chimneys with twist brickwork, peg tiles, exposed timbers and three dormer windows; in one of the bedrooms there were fragments of early decoration – gilded leather and a trompe l'oeil painting on panelling. The large garden had been landscaped in the early twentieth century.

As Gregg walked up the weed-free gravel path between immaculate lawns, he decided that if ever he became wealthy, they'd move from their semidetached to somewhere like this. And Wendy would fill it with beautiful antique furniture with such enthusiasm that they would soon no longer be wealthy.

The heavy oak front door, striated by age, carried a fox's head with a ring through its mouth. He lifted the ring and brought it down on the stud. The sound 'boomed' as it should, speaking of the past.

The door was swung back, with a squeal from its heavy, ancient hinges, and he faced a middle-aged woman, plumpish, dressed for comfort, not fashion; he might have judged her to be a daily help had she not been wearing a large diamond and emerald brooch of obvious quality. 'Mrs Irwin?'

'Yes?'

'I'm Detective Constable Gregg, county police. Your husband requested advice on the level of security of this house.'

'Do come in. I'm afraid he's not here, but perhaps I can tell you what you need to know.' She stepped aside.

He entered.

'I imagine you would like to look over the house?'

'If that is all right?'

'Of course.'

'To begin with, though, I'll need the answers to one or two questions.'

'Then let's go into the sitting room.' She crossed the hall, opened a panelled door, went through the doorway.

The room was full of character – beams, the central one low enough to make him duck his head; inglenook fireplace, with carved initials on the lintel; a small oak side table on which were set four Baccarat paperweights (not that he knew their make; Wendy would have done); an Aubusson rug on the oak flooring (not that he could have named it as such; Wendy would have done); modern, comfortable easy chairs of sufficient quality and design to complement the room rather than appear as ugly intruders. By each chair was a small side table with chequer-banded edges.

They sat. Years ago, he thought, he would not have been received in so friendly a manner. But the possession of wealth no longer provoked a feeling of superiority – except among those who had only recently gained it.

'Now, how can I help you?'

'I understand you have an alarm system already installed?'

'The insurance company insisted on one if they were to continue insuring the contents of the house.'

'Your question is whether it is adequate?'

'There have been so many burglaries – many of our friends have suffered – that my husband has become very worried and thought that since the alarms were put in rather a long time ago, perhaps they were no longer as effective as they should be. Much of what we have is of considerable sentimental value and it would be very distressing to lose it – some of the furniture came through his family and most of my jewellery from my mother. A link to our past.' She paused. 'It's become rather an unsentimental age so I must sound very old-fashioned.'

'Far from it, Mrs Irwin.' Then he added, to show it had not just been a conventional response: 'My wife inherited two rings from her mother and if they were stolen, she would be heartbroken, so I fully understand both your husband's and your worries about security. Has anything specific happened recently to cause you concern?'

'In what way?'

'Has your house recently been brought to public attention by an article in *Country Life* or some other magazine?'

'My husband has never agreed to anything like that.'

'There has been no programme about the house on television?'

'No.'

'In the past few weeks, have you employed someone in the house who suddenly failed to turn up?'

'We have a daily who's been working here for many years and, as far as I know and hope, has no intention of leaving.'

'Have you noticed anyone lurking around here, particularly when you have been out and just returned? Have you noticed more than once the same parked car or van in the road?'

'I don't remember doing so.'

'Has the phone often rung and when the receiver is picked up, the line goes dead?'

'It happens, but I'd never say it does so often.'

'Recently?'

'Not for a while.'

'Has anyone turned up and claimed to be an official who wishes to inspect some aspect of the house?'

'No – only you.'

'Has someone, probably a woman, turned up and said her car's broken down and could she please use your telephone to call for help?'

'Are you asking all these questions because you think someone has been preparing to rob us?'

He hastened to dispel her uneasiness. 'There's no reason

to think that, but these are incidents which can sound the warning that the property is under surveillance. That you have experienced none of them suggests your house has not been targeted.'

'You make it sound like a military exercise.'

'There are times when that might be a just comparison. The military try to learn all they can about where their next action is likely to take place, just as the serious house-breaker always susses his target.'

'Susses?'

'He spends time learning as much about his target as he can. Watches to see if there is a rhythm to the comings and goings of the occupants, judges what will offer the quickest and safest getaway, visually searches for signs of alarms, if a country house, notes where the telephone and electric wires run.'

'I am going to start looking around far more than I do!'

'It is always a good idea to keep a general eye open . . . I think that covers all the initial questions so perhaps now you would show me over the house so that I can inspect the alarm system?'

'If you decide we are not properly protected, will you suggest what we should do?'

'I'll be making out a report for you which will evaluate the current security system and, if necessary, suggest improvements. In that case, I will add a list of firms which are capable of doing the work and have been checked, as far as this can be done, for trustworthiness.'

Ninety-eight minutes later, he left and returned to his car, which was parked outside the large, brick-built garage behind the house. He settled, brought out his notebook from his pocket, checked he had written all that was necessary.

He placed the notebook on the passenger seat, stared through the windscreen. Irwin's fear that the alarm system was not as good as it should be was fully justified. Any reasonably effi-cient team could break in without disturbing anyone; even a mediocre peterman would have the safe – 'hidden' behind one of four framed prints in the main bedroom – open in no time. Querry Brade was a thieves' El Dorado, the valuable contents simply there for the taking.

Gregg frowned to himself and started the engine.

Divisional Headquarters had been built at the beginning of the twentieth century and had long since become unsuitable for its purpose. There had been many requests, even demands, for an up-to-date, purpose-built building, but all had been ignored. Modern society found many more important projects on which to spend money; the police merely maintained law and order.

Gregg climbed the stairs to the fourth floor and went along the dimly lit corridor which always smelled of something, but no one could agree what. CID general room was at the end.

There were six school-type desks, on two of which were computers; all six were strewn with papers and CRO files which had not been locked away in case they were needed quickly. On the right of the door – suffering from woodworm – was a large noticeboard, covered with worn baize, on which were pinned or otherwise fastened lists of official interpreters and night duty officers; computer-enhanced photographs of wanted criminals; details of persons in custody; CID crime information sheets; complaining memos from other departments on which had been added comments, usually of a near obscene nature. By the side of the noticeboard was a battered desk on which were books listing properties searched, the comings and goings of detective constables, personal messages, and the CID crime books.

Gregg checked the crime book. No incident had been recently reported, so no DC had been detailed to a case by the detective inspector. He crossed to his desk, sat, brought out the notebook from his pocket and read what he had written earlier. He wondered how Irwin would respond to the cost of the elaborate system he was going to propose.

Lodge entered the room. A tall man, well built, he had deep blue eyes, a wide forehead, a nose which finished in a slightly upturned end, generous lips and a square, solid chin. He had been very amused, not embarrassed, when, on their first meeting, a girl told him he had mentally undressed her quicker than anyone else ever had. 'Know what I've had to spend my time doing?'

'Sinking a couple of pints of real ale at the Duck and Drake?'

'Trying to find a missing earth-mover.' He slumped down on his chair. 'I ask you, who nicks something that size?'

'Someone who wants earth moved or intends to ease a cash dispenser out of the wall of a bank.'

'It was left on site with no watchman.'

'Maybe the ex-owner is now laughing from ear to ear because it was over-insured.'

'Not judging from his moans of imminent bankruptcy . . . Wasn't there a tractor nicked from a farm near Etlesham some time back?'

'There was.'

'Was it ever traced?'

'It just vanished. Likely, it was in a container and shipped to the Continent before the farmer even knew it was missing.'

'One day, some bright spark will nick Nelson's Column and sell it to the French so they can throw stones at it . . . I've some indexing to do. Would you like to give me a hand?'

'No.'

'As helpful as ever.'

'I've a security report to make out quick sharp.'

'Why the rush?'

'The house is filled with valuable furniture and the wall safe, which is stuffed full of jewellery, wouldn't give an apprentice peterman much trouble.'

'What are you suggesting? Armed guards?'

'Three at each corner . . . The usual, plus changing all locks for top quality ones, a new, much stronger safe, movement, heat, and sound detectors, connected to one of the newly developed electronic transmitter boxes.'

'Which is what?'

'Only just on the market and if they're as good as claimed, they're going to bother chummy. Any sign of movement, rise in temperature, or noise, and the black box is alerted, decides if the cause is human and if so, transmits an alarm by installed mobile phone. So chummy doesn't gain anything but tired wrists from cutting telephone and electricity wires.'

'Isn't all that going to cost a fortune?'

'Shouldn't bother Irwin, and he'll be a fool if it does. The jewellery is valued for insurance at several hundred thousand pounds – one piece is said to have been a tsarina's tiara.'

'Just the bauble a footballer's wife would rush to buy.' Lodge took a pack of cigarettes out of his coat pocket.

'Smoke that in here and you'll be enjoying the hospitality of our cells,' Gregg said humorously.

'I keep forgetting the ban on smoking in public rooms. Bloody government! Forbids us doing what we want to do, makes us do what we don't.'

'They have to show us they're not comatose all the time.' Gregg began to type.

'By the way, you and Wendy are coming to supper.'

'We are?' The interruption had caused him to mistype. He eradicated the word, retyped it. He realized he should have sounded more enthusiastic. 'That's something to look forward to!'

'Guinevere will phone Wendy to fix a day. She'll be cooking a special meal.'

The invitation became even less desirable; their company was enjoyable, her cooking, not.

Two

Wendy was attractive, but not because of her looks. Her hair was an ordinary shade of brown and seldom remained as she wanted; her eyes were an ordinary shade of blue; her nose was a touch too long; there was a mole on her right cheek; her lips were full and shapely, but her chin was a shade too square. She would laughingly say she had been sculpted in a hurry. Yet men would remember her when they had forgotten women who had only recently fired their imaginations. Her attraction lay in her inner warmth, her sense of loyalty, her sympathy for those who had been dealt poor cards by life, a sympathy in which there was no self-congratulation touched with contempt for their lack of success.

As Gregg stepped into the narrow hall, she came out of the kitchen and met him when level with the table on which stood the 1912 ceramic vase whose vivid decoration surely suited the word kitsch. They both disliked it, but it had been given to them as a wedding present and Aunt Kit sometimes visited them and always looked to make certain it was on show. He kissed Wendy, patted her stomach. 'How's junior doing?'

'Kicking.'

'Any sickness?'

'A little.'

Which probably meant a lot. Where she was concerned, morning sickness was misnamed; day-and-night sickness would have been more accurate. Not for the first time, he asked himself why pregnancy and birth had been ordained to mean suffering and pain. Far more reasonable for human reproduction to have resembled that of marsupials. Then, women could have carried their minute young around in cradle bags with designer labels.

'What kind of a day did you have?' she asked, as they drew apart.

'Much as usual. The DI demanded twice as much work as possible, the sarge added more. Still, I escaped most of the hassle. Had to make a security report on a wonderful old house, near Lower Rington, filled with antique furniture which would have made your eyes sparkle with desire.'

'In my present condition? Come into the sitting room and tell me all about it after you've collected a drink for yourself and a sherry for me.'

He hesitated. 'Should . . . They said again on the telly the other day that pregnant women should eschew alcohol.'

'My mother, Mr Andy Gregg, had a glass of whisky every evening when she was carrying me and I arrived whole and yelling. In any case, they keep saying what we shouldn't eat or drink because it's bad for us and six months later they reverse the advice and it's good for us.'

'I doubt they'll soon be advocating whisky for mothers-to-be. However, to hear is to obey. One sherry.'

As she went into the sitting room, he went along the corridor into the kitchen. The small larder was to the side of the back door and the bottom right-hand shelf was their self-christened booze cellar. He poured out a sherry, carried that and a tin of lager into the sitting room, which was homely and comfortable though lacking any piece of antique furniture to gladden Wendy's soul. He handed her the flute, opened the can, sat in the second easy chair.

'Tell me about this wonderful house,' she said.

'Querry Brade. Does the name ring a bell?'

'Never heard it before.'

'The owners are publicity-shy. I'd be the same, if the place were mine. Let the villains get an inkling of what's inside and they'd be queuing up to help themselves.'

'Where is it?'

'Half a mile south of Lower Rington. Carved above the

front door is 1487 and from the look of things, that's a true date, not some owner's wishful imagination. A lovely garden – must take one full-time gardener, at least – and surrounded by open fields.'

He continued to describe his visit and mentioned the furniture and furnishings which had caught his attention; she was unsurprised, yet slightly irritated, when his descriptions were too general to help her identify what he was talking about; before they had met, he had taken no interest in antiques.

'Do they have any children?' she asked.

'None was mentioned, but then there was no reason why any should have been.'

'I hope they do have one or more so they can pass the place on. Houses become warm when they stay in families.'

'And that saves on the central heating.'

'Your humour does not improve.'

'That reminds me. Did Gwen ring you?'

'Gwen Duffey?' she asked with some surprise.

'No   Guinevere.'

'Let her hear you call her Gwen and she'll never speak to you again.'

'You have just placed temptation in my way.'

'She hasn't phoned. Why should she?'

'Sid says she's going to invite us to supper one evening. I'm forgetting. She would have said dinner.'

'Oh dear!'

'That's what I said under my breath – in more robust terms.'

'We'll probably be subjected to the latest recipe on television.'

'Not probably; certainly. Sid says she's going to cook something special.'

'If she'd restrict herself to dishes which need only elementary skill . . . Still, even then it would probably be touch-and-go. I met her yesterday morning in the High Street. But I told you that.'

'Not a word.'

'Yes I did, yesterday evening, but clearly you weren't bothering to listen.'

'You wrong me.'

'I right you. You were reading the paper and weren't going to be interrupted. She insisted on our going to The Lion Hotel for elevenses. They make lousy coffee and charge almost twice as much as anyone else, but she says that's where "the county" go. From the look of who else was there yesterday, one wants to avoid where "the county" go. Have you noticed she's becoming more and more of a grande dame?'

'Can't say I have.'

'Yet Sidney is such an ordinary man and doesn't try to make out he's not far removed from aristocracy.'

'She's been claiming that?'

'Not so far. But you know what I mean. But I'll tell you what, he's become so weak. He won't stand up to her even when she's so obviously wrong.'

'To be happy, a husband learns to accept his wife is always right.'

'Are you so very unhappy? If you went on as he does, I'd almost despise you.'

'We males have very difficult lives. Disagree with one's wife and one's an old-fashioned sexist; agree and one's weak and spineless.'

'Poor you! Don't you think it's odd they married when they're such different characters?'

'Lust is a great spur to ironing out differences.'

'I imagine he played the pack before he met her?'

'He had a wide taste.'

'Yet chose a woman with bitchy instincts.'

'He isn't the first man to have woken up and wondered why he's in bed with the woman by his side.'

'Do you find her sexy?'

'She's attractive.'

'That's not the question.'

'On our first meeting, I thought her a bit run-of-the-mill. Then . . . I don't think I can explain it, but after two or three more meetings, she became quite memorable.'

'Why the change?'

'As I've just said, I don't know. She wasn't all that obvious; didn't wear dresses with very favourable décolleté or skirts so short one hoped she wouldn't sit down gracefully.'

'You are providing a new window into a man's mind.'

'Then I'll stop before it's wide open.'

'There's no room for astonishment! Where did Sidney meet her?'

'At a drinks party.'

'Love at first sight?'

'Lust at first sight. He came back and said he'd met a wench who'd had him panting even before he spoke to her.'

'I thought wolves howled? Does he ever talk to you about her these days?'

'Only generally. He'll tell me they enjoyed a film they saw, where they're hoping to go for their holiday, that sort of thing; nothing personal.'

'She'll want the latest holiday resort for in-people where she can wear a monokini, drink daiquiris, and be surrounded by hungry men.'

'You do dislike her, don't you?'

'There's something of the dark about her. So completely self-centred. Look at the way she treats Sidney. Though he's to blame for allowing her to boss him around.'

'You're hinting you'd rather have much less to do with them?'

'He's a friend who goes way back in your police life and I'm not going to do anything to break up that friendship.'

She had not previously spoken quite so frankly. Since relationships tended to be reciprocal, it was probable that Guinevere disliked her too, despite all her protestations of friendship whenever they met.

She drained her glass. 'I suppose you'll be hard of hearing when I suggest I would like another sherry?'

'Stone deaf.'

'Then you don't have another lager.'

'Since I am not pregnant . . .'

'As a caring husband, you will wish to show your love by altruistically denying yourself as I have to deny myself.'

'Proof, if it were needed, that female logic is totally il-logical,' he said, as he stood and took her glass.

Guinevere and Sidney had recently settled in bed.

'I was walking down East Street this morning and chanced to look into the window of Mandy and Rill,' she said.

'Who?'

'The jewellers.'

'We were called there a few weeks back.'

'You know I like bats?'

'Always thought women were afraid of them because they become tangled in long hair which then has to be cut off to free them.'

'That's a myth. When I lived at home, we had bats in the attic.'

'Not in the belfry?' He chuckled.

She pinched him.

'That hurt!'

'Maybe it will teach you not to make silly jokes. You're like Andy, who's forever making stupid puns. It nearly drives Wendy crazy.'

'Wouldn't have thought anything would do that, she's so calm and collected.'

'Stolid.'

'Don't you think . . .?'

'When I was still living in the country, I was sitting outside because it was such a warm night and there was a crescent moon. I was feeling sad . . .'

'Why?'

'Do you have to keep interrupting me?'

'Sorry.'

'I looked up and saw a bat fly across the moon. I became certain something wonderful was about to happen to cheer me up because bats are good luck.'

He would have liked to ask her who or what suggested that, but remained silent, unwilling to aggravate her.

'Don't you want to know what my good luck was?'

'Of course I do.'

'I met you.'

He was astonished, being more used to complaints than compliments. If she was in that good a mood . . . He kissed her.

After a while, she drew her head back. 'The moment I saw it, I knew it had to have been made for me, for us. So we would have all the good luck in the world.' She waited. 'Aren't you interested?'

'Very much, only . . .'

'Well?'

'I'm not quite certain what you're talking about.'

'The brooch.'

'What brooch?'

'For God's sake, do you have to be so thick? The one in Mandy and Rill's show window. It was on a stand covered in black velvet and looked incredibly beautiful. There's the crescent moon, which is good luck, and the bat, which means even better luck, flying across it, with its wings touching the tips of the crescent. I could have gone straight in and bought it.'

'What's it made of?'

'Silver, gold, and diamonds.'

'Then it's a good job you didn't.'

'Why say that?'

'It must cost a packet.'

'It's a designer piece, so there won't be another like it. I'm sure that on me it would look absolutely stunning. Darling, we can buy it, can't we?'

'Not unless we win the lottery.'

'It's only two thousand.'

'Pounds or pence?'

'You're being stupid again. It's just no good talking to you.' She turned on to her side, her back facing him.

'But you know we have to think twice about spending two thousand pence right now because of all the debts.'

'I suppose you're going to start going at me again for buying clothes. You won't understand I want to look nice, not like the wife of a down-at heels.'

'I know you do, I love seeing you dressed smartly, but we do owe rather a lot of money.'

'You won't buy the brooch for me?'

'It's impossible.'

'I do everything you want to make you happy and get nothing in return. All right, if that's your attitude, I won't bother to make you happy.'

'Can't you understand?'

She switched off her light.

He stroked her back. 'I'd do anything I could for you. You know that.'

'Do I? When you've just refused to do anything?'

'Two thousand pounds is—'

'No more than you'd have to pay on the streets for what you get from me for free. Leave me alone.'

He stared up at the ceiling. She had spent much more, on clothes and accessories, than they could afford and only his unofficial earnings kept their financial heads above water. There was no way they could suffer a further debt of £2,000. Yet if they didn't, experience told him she would deny him her body while doing everything to bring it to his attention.

He slept fitfully. He awoke at five and by some strange alchemy of the brain knew how to find the £2,000.

He edged across the bed and pressed his body against hers. She stirred.

'I've something to tell you, darling.'

'Leave me alone,' she mumbled.

'Do you think the jewellers would hold the brooch for us for a couple of weeks?'

'Why?'

'Maybe we could find the money.'

She turned over to face him. 'You really mean that?'

'Hand on heart.'

'Then why don't you put your hand somewhere else?'

Three

A week after the security survey of Querry Brade, Denton parked the Astra – stolen three hours previously and chosen for its ubiquity – in the small natural clearing just inside the woods. It was unlikely to be observed from the road, especially since it was after midnight, but if by mischance it was, the onlooker would probably presume that a couple were getting to know each other.

Rutter climbed out of the front of the car, a hold-all in his hand, Tobin out of the back; Denton stayed behind the wheel. His task was to wait and to come to their aid if called by mobile and it became necessary to drive like hell after he'd picked them up.

Rutter spoke through the opened window. 'If I call, you come round to the front of the house.'

'Yeah, yeah, you said.'

They were experienced, yet still suffered tension when on a job.

Rutter and Tobin drew lengths of nylon stocking over their heads. Considered yesterday's disguise by many, it was the best when there had to be unencumbered head mobility. Tobin, very heavily built but light of movement, carrying two blankets led the way up the ride, treading carefully because the moon was bright enough to provide direction, but not the details of the ground. Behind him, Rutter cursed as he stumbled and almost fell after catching his foot on a length of rotting wood. Clumsy sod, Tobin thought. He held Rutter in both contempt and respect. Contempt for physical weakness; respect for skill.

The drive began a wide sweep which ended at a five-bar

gate. They opened this, went into a field in which cattle, dimly seen, regarded them with calm interest. Rutter cursed again as he stepped in a cowpat. Tobin laughed sarcastically.

A yew hedge surrounded the garden. At the southern end of this was a gate. Tobin moved aside to allow Rutter to check for outside alarms, even though they had been told there was none. Rutter ran his fingers, in surgical gloves, over the gate and the gateposts as he sought any break in the surfaces to suggest an unreported alarm.

He signalled the gate was safe and moved back. Ready to run at the first sound of an alarm, Tobin decided. They approached the side of the house since there were motion-activated lights at front and back. There were three ground-floor windows, unevenly spaced. Rutter put down his hold-all in front of the centre one, opened it, brought out a torch with adjustable shutters now set at their minimum to allow little more than a pinpoint beam. He switched it on, handed it to Tobin to shine at the right-hand middle bottom pane of glass.

After spreading out one of the blankets on the ground, Rutter used a glass cutter to describe a circle in the pane. Since the glass could only be pulled out by pressure from the inside, he forced a thin, tapered steel rod through the putty and under the glass. He applied pressure on the rod which acted as a lever on the interior. The glass fractured along the lines of the cut and the circle fell out on to the blanket. Tobin flipped the glass on to the lawn, unfolded the second and larger blanket and held it over the window to stifle any light.

Rutter ducked under the blanket and with the torch shutters now wide open, visually examined the sill, sides and top frame. Wires had not been embedded and they ran along the right-hand side. A compass, placed against the wiring, showed no deflection, indicating it was an open, not a closed circuit. The report had said security was poor. It should, Rutter told himself, have been termed virtually non-existent. He reached in and cut the wires. A very thin, strong length of steel forced back the catch between the two halves of the sash window; very slow and careful pressure raised the lower one with no discernible sound.

Rutter climbed over the sill. Tobin passed him the blankets before following. They were in the dining room. Against one wall was a George III serpentine sideboard; in the centre of the room a George III D-end table with eight square, tapering legs; on it stood a George I pepper pot and salt caster; around it were eight Sheraton mahogany chairs. Rutter knew they were looking at a fortune, but furniture was trouble to transport, silver of great quality usually too well documented to be readily sold.

The plan of the house was rough, but accurate. The flight of stairs had a balustraded half-landing from which a tall man could look part of the way down the upstairs corridor. All was quiet. The master bedroom lay to the right. They moved carefully along the heavily carpeted, wooden floor to the first door on their right.

Tobin flung the panelled wooden door back with the force to crash it against the wall. Since it was hinged to the right, he reached to the left for light switches, depressed them, crossed to the side of the oak tester bed where Heather Irwin had been sleeping until shocked awake, leaving her muddle-headed. Irwin, recovering more quickly, began to move. Tobin held a spring-loaded cosh above her head. When Irwin froze, his face contorted with fear for his wife, Rutter went round to his side of the bed, produced plastic bonds – official issue – motioned to him to put out his hands, wrists together. Irwin did not move. Tobin swung the cosh down, just missing the side of her head. Heather screamed. Irwin held out his hands and they were secured.

Tobin pulled back the bedclothes, secured Irwin's legs, went back round the bed. Heather's nightdress had risen up over her thighs and as he approached, she tried to pull it down. He grabbed her wrists, secured them, then her legs.

Rutter, satisfied there would be no opposition, crossed the room to the four framed prints on the wall, swung back the far end one. The wall safe had a combination lock.

Given time, with the right equipment, he might have solved the combination, but there was no need for such arcane expertise. He used a small, heavily loaded hammer to knock off the dial, a punch to force the spindle back; he broke the sockets, pulled the door open.

There were five large jewel boxes, several smaller ones. Rutter brought out a large one, opened it, and greedily stared at the rings, set out in a velvet-covered holder. If all the boxes were equally well loaded, they were making themselves a fortune.

They left the bedroom and made their way downstairs. Rutter, his nature perverse, hated those from whom he stole because they were wealthy enough to make it worth his while to steal from them. He used the loaded hammer to reduce one of the chairs in the dining room to rubble.

Four

S oon after six, Irwin managed to free himself following hours of painful movement – roll off the bed on to the floor, try and fail to dial 999 with his nose, wriggle across to the door and along the landing, descend the stairs in a series of thumps which threatened to end in one long fall, more wriggling to the kitchen, over a quarter of an hour to get upright, almost as long to open a drawer, extract a knife with teeth, clamp it between knees, begin to cut through the plastic securing the wrists, drop the knife, start all over again, then finally, with muscles painful, cramp even more so, freedom.

He released his wife, dialled 999, asked for an ambulance before reporting the break-in and assault. He returned to her side and rubbed her wrists and ankles to restore life to them; he quietly assured her that help was on its way. Because she was shaking and murmuring incomprehensibly, he feared that although she had suffered little physical harm, shock had mentally disturbed her badly.

A police patrol car arrived a couple of minutes before an ambulance. Heather Irwin was examined briefly by the medico who advised Irwin that his wife should be taken to hospital to be examined by someone more qualified than he. Conscious of Irwin's panicky concern, he added that he thought it likely her full recovery would be a matter of time and quiet, nothing more.

Irwin watched the ambulance drive away. He spoke abruptly to the PC who had been the only occupant of the patrol car. 'I need a drink before I go to the hospital.' PC Tyler mundanely wondered whether to advise against drinking and driving, decided there were times when such advice was good, but contrary to nature. He followed Irwin into the sitting room.

'What will you have?'

'Nothing, thank you.'

Irwin crossed to an attractive, inlaid cocktail cabinet which managed to look as if it were made before cocktails were invented, poured himself a large whisky, drank quickly. 'Shakes a man up a bit.'

'Very much so, sir.' The PC was normally parsimonious with his 'sirs' – it was an age of equality – but he admired Irwin for the way in which he was coping with the emotional fears he had suffered. A figure of amusement, an old buffer to many because of his manner and accented speech, yet possessed of an inner strength which so many now lacked. Suggest he be offered counselling and he would regard acceptance as weakness.

Irwin poured himself a second whisky, crossed to a chair, sat. 'We were both fast asleep. Woken by the door crashing open and the lights going on. Two men in the bedroom with some sort of netting over their heads. One had a hold-all . . .'

'It will be best if you wait to tell CID what happened, Mr Irwin. They'll be here very soon.'

Irwin might not have heard. 'The large one was a brute of a man. Couldn't see either of their faces because of the netting over them, but he was a thug all right. Know what I mean?'

'Unfortunately, all too readily.'

'They made it clear that something terrible would happen to my wife if I tried to stop them. But for that, I would have done.'

And been severely injured or murdered, Tyler thought.

'Can't understand how they reached the bedroom without waking one or both of us. The stairs creak and we're light sleepers. Tied us up. The wife's nightdress was up, but they didn't have the decency to pull it down.'

Tyler surmised that for the moment, this incident weighed as heavily on Irwin's mind as the theft.

'Then one of them went over to the end print, swung it back, and opened the safe. Took everything. All the jewellery, much of which came down through the family. Hurts.'

And for someone of his nature, the insurance money – assuming they had full insurance – would not ease the loss.

'I must drive to the hospital and see how she is.'

'I'm afraid you'll have to wait until CID arrives. But why not phone and ask them?' The two large whiskies made driving definitely inadvisable. 'And as soon as it's OK, I'll drive you there.'

'You will? Damned decent of you.'

The phone awoke Gregg.

'What . . . Who?' Wendy mumbled.

He reached out and picked up the receiver of the bedside telephone, put it to his ear.

'Is that you, Andy?'

'Who the hell do you expect it to be?' he answered with sleepy resentment.

'Get out to Lower Rington and a home called Querry Brade.'

The name jerked his mind wide awake. 'Christ! What's happened there?'

'Two men broke in and helped themselves to a fortune in jewellery; the wife's been taken off to hospital – shock, not physical injury. The skipper wants you out there five minutes ago.'

Gregg replaced the receiver, climbed out of bed.

'Trouble?' Wendy muttered.

'A bad break-in.'

He dressed rapidly, went to kiss her goodbye and found she had already fallen asleep. He switched off the light as he left the bedroom.

Detective Inspector Horton was not his usual smoothly presented self. He had only roughly combed his hair, his chin was stubbled, his shirt was tieless, he wore an old sweater despite his wife's insistence that he was not leaving the house looking like a tramp.

He braked to a halt behind two other cars in front of Querry Brade. As he approached the portico, a PC stepped out of the nearer one. 'You want something?'

'Detective Inspector Horton.'

'Sorry, sir, didn't recognize you.'

Maybe he did look like a tramp. 'You are?'

'Tyler. Vehicles. I was directed by Ops because I was patrolling nearby.'

'Who else is here?'

'Three or four, sir.'

'Then what's been holding you back from returning to duty?'

Horton's reputation had him as sharp as a butcher's knife. 'I was with Mr Irwin after the ambulance left. He had a couple of drinks and talked to me before I drove him to be with his wife in hospital. Reckoned I'd best come back to report what he said to me, but the sarge said I was to stand by until CID arrived.'

'A man of initiative.'

Tyler was unsure whether that was praise or sarcasm.

Horton stepped into the hall, waited for Tyler to join him. 'What did Mr Irwin tell you?'

Tyler began to repeat the evidence Irwin had given him.

'Once they were secured in bed, the smaller of the two men went directly over to the end framed print? He didn't look around the bedroom first?'

'Not according to what Mr Irwin said.'

'Probably had had a shufty before they woke them up.'

'They're both light sleepers and it was the bedroom door being thrown open and the light going on which woke them.'

'I need to hear the rest of the story. Tell Ops you're to remain here.'

The forensic squad were conducting their investigation to even Horton's satisfaction. All possible surfaces had been, or were being, checked for prints; the bedroom was being finger-searched; the safe had been photographed, as had been the plastic restraints; the route it was presumed the thieves had taken from the dining room to the master bedroom had already been double-checked; outside, the circle of glass, unbroken as it had landed on grass, had been recovered; the area of ground around the window had been finger-searched; the window had been intensely examined . . .

Horton yawned as he entered the sitting room. Tyler had been dozing, slumped sideways in the chair, and he hastily sat upright, stood.

'Sit down and tell me from the beginning what you heard from Mr Irwin,' Horton said as he settled on a chair.

Tyler cleared his throat, then made his report with the same careful formality with which he would have presented evidence in court.

'Let's go back again to the moment they entered the bedroom.'

'Mr Irwin awoke to see the bigger man approach his side of the bed and the smaller one putting a hold-all down on the floor. When Mr Irwin didn't instantly put out his hands to be secured, the bigger man slammed a cosh down by the side of his wife's head. When they had been tied up, the smaller man went over to the end framed print and swung it back to reveal the safe.'

'He went directly to the end one?'

'That's what was said.'

Horton fingered his jaw, a habit of his which greatly annoyed his wife.

Gregg awoke and for a brief moment feared that the sunlight reaching between the drawn curtains meant he had over-slept. Reason returned. He climbed out of bed, had a shower, dressed and went downstairs.

Wendy, who had been cleaning the table in the small alcove, did not look up.

'I slept like the dead, but am now back to life and ready, if not very willing, to return to work.'

'Do you want something to eat before you leave?'

Her manner disturbed him. Her normal greeting had been absent and her tone suggested resentment. 'Eggs and bacon, please.'

She brought a saucepan out of the nearby cupboard and put it on the stove, poured vegetable oil into it, lit the gas underneath. She brought two eggs and a pack of bacon out of the refrigerator.

He cut two slices of bread and dropped them into the toaster.

'Love, is something wrong?' he asked.

'Why ask?'

'You're behaving as if I'm halfway to the doghouse.'

'That surprises you?'

'Come on, out with it. What am I guilty of?'

'It's Sunday.'

'I'm not responsible for that.'

'It was your Sunday off.'

'You know that if something big breaks, even if it is off-time, I have to turn up and—'

She interrupted him. 'Do you remember what we were going to do?'

'Of course.'

'What?'

He had forgotten, so spoke as confidently as possible. 'A meal out, the cinema, a visit to a friend, depending.'

'We were going to have a picnic by the sea provided only that it wasn't too cold or raining. The forecast is the day's going to be warm and sunny.'

'Look, we'll do that my next free day.'

'If there's no emergency?'

'There won't be. I guarantee that.'

'It won't be the same.'

'No, it'll be even better. The sea will be like a warm bath because there will be tropical sunshine.'

The interior of the toaster sprang up and he withdrew two pieces of toast, buttered them, carried the plate across to the stove.

'I suppose,' she said distantly, 'I shouldn't be surprised you can't remember anything about it.' She used a slice to transfer egg and bacon on to the toast.

'I'm never at my sharpest before morning coffee.'

'No. Very blunt.'

'I know it's disappointing . . .'

'Not nearly as disappointing as you not knowing *why* it's disappointing.'

'How's that?'

'Suppose you eat before it gets cold?'

'I'd rather have cold eggs and bacon than you acting like I've irredeemably disgraced myself with a blonde.'

'Three years ago today, I said I'd like to go on a picnic and you told me you knew just the place where we'd be away from the crowds, yet by the sea. So we had a picnic where you'd suggested. Can you remember that much?'

He made an indeterminate sound.

'Of course not. So if I added that was the day and place you proposed to me, it would come as a guilty surprise? Or perhaps you would not feel the slightest guilt about missing so unimportant a day?' She turned off the gas, walked past him and out of the kitchen.

He carried his plate over to the small table, sat, did not begin to eat but stared into space. At one time or another, police work strained every marriage; criminal activity repeatedly caused the last-minute cancellation of social plans. Wendy had accepted that – until now. Because of her pregnancy? She was being very unfair. How many husbands three years after their marriage could remember the date and place of their engagement?

Five

Trentford was not somewhere often remembered with pleasure. The roads were narrow; parking was expensive and severely restricted; supermarkets and chain stores had driven away almost all of the small shops which had offered personal service; the commemorative statue for WWI and WWII had been moved to the edge of the town where few saw it because it had been causing traffic problems when in the centre; and the newly elected mayor wore the chain of office whenever he could summon reason for doing so.

The traffic was unusually heavy and caused Gregg to take twenty-five minutes to drive to Querry Brade. He parked behind other cars, went into the house, met Horton when halfway across the hall.

'Kind of you to honour us with your presence.'

When Horton indulged in childish sarcasm, it was a signal that he was in a bloody-minded mood.

'Since you've finally managed to arrive, you can go into the sitting room where Mr Irwin is waiting. Tell him I'll be there as soon as I can be.' He hurried to the staircase.

Gregg crossed the hall, opened the door of the sitting room, went inside. Irwin, his oval face expressing strain, looked up.

'Detective Constable Gregg, sir.'

Irwin nodded, stared at the far wall, suddenly came to his feet. 'Very sorry. I'm afraid events have disturbed me rather more than I thought. I believe you've met my wife?'

'Yes, I have.'

'Most unfortunately, the advice you gave us has been of

no effect because the firm, whom we contacted, promised to do the work right away, but did not.'

'Terribly bad luck . . . Inspector Horton will be here in a minute and asks you to be kind enough to wait so that he can have a word with you.'

'Of course. Do sit down.'

Gregg settled on the same chair as on his previous visit. 'How is your wife?'

'Much better and according to the specialist will be able to come home soon.'

'I'm glad to hear that.'

'Terrible experience for her.'

'It must have been very frightening for both of you.'

There was a silence.

'They took all the jewellery. Some of it had been in my wife's family for two or three generations. The tiara was worn by her aunt and so was the baroque pearl sea horse. Her husband used to say that every time he walked down Bond Street or Regent Street with her, he was hundreds of pounds the poorer . . . I'm boring you, of course.'

'No, sir.'

'Nothing worse than listening to family histories when you don't know the people. But losing all that jewellery and the senseless smashing of the chair . . .'

Horton entered the room. 'Sorry to have delayed you, Mr Irwin, but I had to sort something out.' He nodded at Gregg, who had stood, to sit, went across to a chair.

'I was boring Mr Gregg by telling him about the jewellery,' Irwin said.

'I am sure he was far from bored. I am afraid I have to ask you questions which are going to bring back memories that are bound to distress you. I'll be as brief as possible.'

'What are the chances of your retrieving the jewellery?'

'Very difficult to say at this stage. All that is certain is that we will be doing all we can to recover everything.'

'Should I offer a reward?'

'That could well help, however my advice is to have a word with your insurance company.'

'Very well.'

'I'd like you to tell us every single thing you can remember from the moment the villains entered your bedroom. Nothing will be too insignificant. Even the unusual way in which a man walks could help.'

Irwin spoke slowly. He had known nothing until the door crashed open and the light went on . . . 'Damned if I can understand why I didn't hear them coming upstairs. I'm a very light sleeper.'

'Some of them seem to be able to walk on air. Will you describe the two men?'

'Their faces were obscured with what I thought was netting. I've been told it was probably nylon stocking.'

'Very likely. Were they big, small, medium, fat, thin? Was there anything about their builds which attracted your attention? As far as you could judge, did either have an unusually shaped head? Did they move easily with no sign of a limp?'

Irwin replied that in his shocked state, he had noticed little. All he could say for certain was that one man had been considerably larger than the other . . . 'Lying there, helpless, knowing I couldn't help her . . . I hope to God I never have to go through anything like that again.'

'I am certain you won't. How would you judge their heights?'

'I suppose the bigger man was six feet or slightly more and built like a bull. The smaller man, rather thin, and three or four inches shorter.'

'Was there anything about their hands which drew your attention?'

'They were both wearing some kind of plastic glove.'

'Who was giving the orders?'

'The smaller man, but he never spoke. Neither of them did. Just used signals to each other as well as to us.'

'It was the smaller man who forced the safe?'

'Yes.'

'How do you think he knew where it was?'

'I don't quite understand . . .?'

'Had they first searched your bedroom, looking for a safe?'

'No.'

'Then they entered, switched on the light, and once your wife and you were helpless, walked straight across to the print at the end on the wall?'

'That's right.'

'Can you be certain that's what happened? This is a very important point and when someone is under great stress, as you were, memory can be mistaken.'

'I am quite certain that after the other man had slammed the cosh down by my wife's head, he went over to the end print and swung it back.'

'Was he right- or left-handed?'

'I don't know.'

'You've said the two did not speak, but used signs. Was there any moment when one of them did actually speak a word or two?'

'No.'

Horton stood, walked over to the window, stared out at the garden. Irwin, perplexed, said, 'I'm saying how I remember things. I'm perfectly prepared to accept I must be wrong.'

Horton returned to the chair. 'I should like to believe you are. I don't think you are. Did it take the second man long to open the safe?'

'Not nearly long enough, considering what I paid for it.' For the first time, Irwin showed a trace of humour.

'You might have paid twice as much and still have lost everything. There are one or two petermen who are skilful enough to keep the Bank of England awake at nights . . . Can you describe how he opened it?'

'His back was to me and I was watching the large man for fear . . . for fear he would assault my wife sexually. But he hammered something which fell to the floor, then he hit something else and there was a change of tune.'

'Pushing the spindle back and breaking the sockets. It is sharp of you to be able to distinguish the two actions . . .

You'll be very glad, Mr Irwin, to hear that I don't need to ask you anything more right now. Thank you for your co-operation and my apologies for having to provoke unwanted memories.' He stood.

'You do think there's a good chance you'll be able to retrieve the jewellery?'

'A very reasonable chance.' He had answered more positively than before. Hope could be a solace and he was not always indifferent to the feelings of others – unless they were under his command.

'I gather you want a word, sir?' Detective Sergeant Warren said gloomily (indeed, he was a gloomy man) as he entered the detective inspector's room on Monday morning.

'Half an hour ago.'

It was only five minutes since he had received the summons, but it was not advisable to point that out. Horton did not like being corrected by his juniors.

'Sit.'

As Warren settled, he wondered if he had done something he should not or had not done something he should. The DI had an evil ability to identify mistakes, however small or in practical terms irrelevant. He gave perfectionism a new meaning.

Horton had been working on his computer. He clicked the mouse and the printer started. He sat back. 'I was at Querry Brade for much of yesterday. Things appear to be going smoothly, but slowly.'

'It's going to be tough, sir, because the two villains were obviously old hands.'

'Long-term partners?'

'I wouldn't think so. These days, the planner usually picks the players for the specific job.'

'If you'd been planning this one, wouldn't you have called for more than two men to be in the house?'

'Do we know there weren't any others?'

'We can't be certain, but that seems likely.'

'Then they must have decided two would be sufficient.'

'How could they have decided that?'

'From the usual observations.'

'Gregg asked Mrs Irwin if they had noticed any of the signs of that and her reply was they had not.'

'Doesn't mean she was right.'

'The villains knew it was going to be a simple break-in.'

The printer stopped working. Horton collected two sheets of paper and set them up in front of himself. 'I questioned Mr Irwin yesterday.'

'So I heard.'

'The villains burst into the bedroom, tied them up, and the smaller man went straight over to the end print on the wall and swung it back to reveal the safe. There was no search for it.' He picked up a pencil and began to doodle. 'The burglary took place only days after the Irwins had been advised of the need for a much more advanced security system because the existing one was next to useless. Odd, would you say?'

'Coincidence.'

'Had the villains waited a few days, the new system would have been installed and they'd have found the job very much more difficult; perhaps even too much for them.'

'Then they were lucky.'

'Luck can be the result of seeing a chance and seizing it.'

'Don't see the difference. It's luck to be able to see the chance.'

'When a couple of men break into a house looking for loot, what's their initial move?'

'Bit difficult to answer . . .'

'In a big house, the search for a safe can take a long time, yet every minute they're inside is dangerous, so the quickest way of finding it is to get hold of the owner and force him, perhaps through threatening his wife, to disclose where it is. These lads didn't act like that. As soon as the Irwins were secured, the peterman went straight over to the four framed prints and swung back the end one. He must have known the safe was there.'

'I don't see that, sir. Rich people live in big houses and rich wives have jewellery which they often keep in a safe in their bedroom so as it's close by and they can gloat over what's inside.'

'I repeat, he went directly to the end print.'

'Chance.'

'He was certain the safe was there,' Horton said for the second time.

'You're saying the villains were tipped off by someone who works in the house?'

'That's one possibility, but the Irwins don't, as one might think, have a large staff – likely they're capital rich but relatively income poor. There's just one daily who's been with them for years and, if you accept their judgment, beyond suspicion. The garden is looked after by contract.'

'Maybe the firm who installed the safe employed someone who's bent.'

'A second possibility. So speak to the firm and find out if they've anyone with whom we're familiar on their books. There is another possibility, isn't there?'

Warren resented what was being implied. 'The Irwins have loud mouths and talked too much.'

'Very unlikely, judging by the care with which they have made certain the house has received no publicity.'

'Then I'm stumped.'

Warren, Horton thought, had recognized what the fourth possibility must be, but could not accept it. 'Gregg's report made it obvious a robbery at Querry Brade would be a very profitable one and, until the new security system had been installed, an easy one. The report describes the existing security and its weaknesses in detail and in doing so provides a good layout of the house.'

'You're suggesting the villains got a sight of the report?'

'That seems probable.'

'Then the Irwins did leak it. They must have shown it to someone who wasn't as tight-lipped as they are.'

'The source is more likely to be here.'

Warren's response was loud. 'Impossible!'

Jeffrey Ashford

'Unfortunately, not so.'

'It's ridiculous to suggest anyone here would sell information.'

'It happens.'

'Elsewhere, maybe, but not in our team, not in our division. You have to be wrong.'

'Who has been in a position to be able to feed the villains with information?'

'No one.'

'Gregg carried out the survey and wrote the report. Because of the obvious danger of a security report reaching criminal hands, he's ordered to take every precaution to make certain no one else, even in the CID room, can read what is in his computer; access to it is restricted to him. That's right, isn't it?'

'Yes, but—'

'If he stuck to the rules, he first prints out one copy of his report and that is passed to you and to me for comment. If alterations are required, these are made and the revised report is printed twice while the original is shredded. One remains here, under lock and key, the other is handed to the Irwins. That means only three people here should be in a position to be able to sell the information.'

'Are you accusing me – *sir*?' Warren added after a pause, making the word of respect, disrespectful.

'I am not. Nor have I spoken about it to anyone. Which leaves Gregg.'

'I'd trust him absolutely, however much the facts are twisted.'

'Nothing has been twisted.'

'They are assumptions, not facts.'

'Yet logical assumptions. Which is why we are going to have to prove them right or wrong.'

Six

Detective Constable Chappell had rugged features, red hair, red beard, and the build of a rugger forward, yet in contrast to the initial impression his appearance created, he was far from aggressive, often changed his son's nappies to ease his wife's work, and played the violin in a local orchestra.

He knocked on the front door of a terrace house which showed many signs of neglect. When there was no response, he knocked again with sufficient force to make the flap of the letterbox rattle.

The door was finally opened by Edna Swift. A petite woman with attractive features, naturally curling, naturally blonde hair, and a body shaped for the catwalk, she dressed cheaply, but with enough taste that one might have been mistaken and thought her clothes were expensive. Months before, Chappell had had reason to speak to her and on his return to the CID room, had said, 'How could a woman that sharp marry a squint like Swift?' The question had left him wide open to rough humour. 'Penny married you, didn't she?'

'Hullo, Edna,' he said.

'What is it this time?' she demanded in her husky voice.

'I need a chat with Perce.'

'He ain't here.'

'Working in daylight?'

There was a shout from upstairs, loud enough to reach outside. 'Who is it?'

'That sounds like Perce,' Chappell said, 'but if he's not here, I suppose it's the plumber come to check your plumbing.'

Her expression darkened.

'Mind if I come in?'

'Yes.'

'Lighten up, Edna.'

'Bastards.'

'I'm told that at least one of us may have traditional parents . . . Work it out. Surely it's kinder to your reputation with the neighbours to allow me to come in now, all quietly, than have flashing cars and a squad on the warpath turn up?'

She turned, walked down the short passage and through an opened doorway, slammed the door shut behind her.

As he stepped into the hall, there was another shout.

'Who the bleeding hell is it?'

'I'm asking for a contribution to the organization for the preservation of old lags.'

From upstairs came the sound of quick movement, from beyond the far downstairs door, the clatter of dishes. The hall, with all doors closed, was in gloom until an unshaded overhead light was switched on.

Swift came down the stairs. He was short, overweight, and balding; to describe him as merely ill-featured was being generous. 'Morning, Mr Chappell,' he said, as he reached the floor.

'It warms my heart to find it wasn't the plumber.'

'How's that?'

'Edna said you were out.'

'Must have thought I was.'

'Easy mistake to make.'

'You was wanting something, Mr Chappell?'

'A chat.'

'What about?'

'Suppose we move to somewhere where we can be comfortable before I explain?'

Swift looked at the front door, then round at the kitchen door; accepting fate, he led the way into the front room, which was well decorated and furnished and in stark contrast to the dismal hall. They sat on easy chairs which faced a

25-inch flat-screen TV and a blanked-out fireplace. On the mantelpiece was a line of miniature cats; on the settee, a live Siamese regarded Chappell with aristocratic indifference.

Swift moved uneasily, coughed, looked at Chappell, hastily away. The silence began to unnerve him. 'You was going to say what you wanted.'

'I did. A chat.'

'You ain't said what about.'

'You don't need me to tell you that.'

'Straight, I don't know.'

'Innocence doesn't become you.'

'I swear I ain't been busy.'

'Just working gently?'

'I ain't touched anything in months. Edna said she wasn't staying if I went inside again.'

'The power of true love!'

Swift picked up a pack of cigarettes from the small table by his side, brought one out with fingers that trembled. He lit the cigarette, inhaled, suddenly said, 'Sorry, Mr Chappell. Didn't think to offer you one.'

'Gave up smoking some time back.'

'Edna goes on at me about it. I've tried to give up, but before I knows what's happening, there's a fag in me mouth and she's raising hell. I tell her, I didn't mean to smoke, it just happened, but she don't listen.'

'Quite right of her. Smoking is very non-PC these days. I want to hear where you were Saturday night, very early Sunday morning.'

'Saturday?'

'Saturday.'

'I was here.'

'Why?'

'I like the telly.'

'Because it teaches you about all the big houses stuffed full of goodies, like Querry Brade?'

'You don't . . .'

'Don't what?'

'Think I had anything to do with that job?'

'Can't say I find the thought difficult. Quite a haul. One of the pieces is said to be from a Russian tiara . . . But, of course, you know that.'

'How could I?'

'By reading the papers. You could do yourself a lot of good, returning it. A judge will look more kindly on a peterman with sufficient soul to return a historically important tiara, rather than break it up, rip out the stones, and melt down the metal.'

'I ain't done a job since I last left the nick.'

'But that was over a year and a half ago.'

'It don't matter if it was yesterday.'

'If that were so, you'd be right out in the clear.'

'I promised Edna.'

'They say nothing's easier than making a promise, nothing more difficult than keeping it.'

'I was here.'

'You realize you're trying to tell me there's someone out there as sharp with a peter as you? I'd find believing in fairies easier.'

'It couldn't have been me. Ask Edna,' Swift said frantically.

'I wouldn't expect her to sacrifice you with the truth.'

'She'll tell you it couldn't of been me.'

'The description of the peterman who forced the safe as easily as brushing his hair fits you as snugly as your cat's skin fits it.'

'I can prove it wasn't me.'

'Then what's been holding you back?'

'You know my form, don't you?'

'So long, it took me hours to plough through it before coming here.'

'Have I ever used violence?'

'You've never been charged and convicted of it.'

'Violence scares me.'

'Mostly it's the victim gets scared.'

He spoke in a rush of words. 'My old man used to beat the shit out of my mum when he was tight. When I was a kid, seeing her punched and kicked, screaming, frightened me silly. I couldn't hit a woman, not if it was to escape you lot. The paper said they threatened to smash the wife if there was any trouble from the husband and one of 'em was by her bed to do it. I couldn't be in on that.'

'It wasn't the peterman who made the threats and stood ready to carry them out if necessary.'

'I couldn't have worked in that team . . . You've got to understand. Them threatening her like they did, proves it wasn't me.'

'Sorry, Perce, but it doesn't prove anything. So the best thing is for you to come on down to the station and make a statement.'

'Then she'll say I've been picked up because you lot reckon I was on that job in the house you talked about.'

'How could she think that when according to what you've just told me, you were with her all the night?'

'She'll likely leave me.'

'More likely, you'll be leaving her for a few years.'

'I was here,' he said yet again.

'No, you weren't, or you wouldn't be afraid of Edna thinking you'd been busy. Let's start moving so as I can have my lunch before it's supper time.'

'She . . .'

'What?'

'Don't like me boozing.'

'Few wives do. They lack understanding.'

'I told her I'd been with friends only I was out boozing.'

'Out until when?'

'Can't rightly remember.'

'You're sounding less and less convincing.'

'I was too far gone to know what the time was.'

'Edna will be able to tell me.'

'She sleeps so heavy I got in without waking her.'

'You weren't singing to celebrate the neat job you'd just pulled off?'

'I was just boozing.'

'Name the people you were with.'

'When I've a pint or two inside me, I don't remember nothing.'

'That's bad luck for you!'

'You've got to believe me.'

'Sorry, Perce, but some tasks are just too difficult.'

Swift became even more frantic. 'You don't have to take me in. I'll make the statement here.'

'I need it to be all official so your mouthpiece can't say in court that I beat it out of you with a baseball bat.'

'Look, if you was willing to . . .'

'I'm not.'

His tone became wheedling. 'I could do you a good turn.'

'Are you trying to offer me a quid pro quo?'

'Wouldn't know about that.'

'What's the information?'

'I ain't saying until you lay off me.'

'Then on your feet and start walking.'

Swift hesitated, finally said, 'There's someone selling information.'

'Happens all the time and mostly it's not worth the price.'

'This is different.'

'How?'

'The job you've been on about.'

'Well?'

'It was easy.'

'I don't need anyone to tell me that.'

'The boys had all the information about the job.'

'Name them.'

'And get me throat cut?'

Chappell stood. 'What you've been telling isn't worth a spit. Get moving.'

'The information was sold by a copper. The boys knew the job would be easy if it was done quick before fresh security was put in.'

Chappell delivered a brief, contemptuous, sulphurous opinion of anyone who so lacked intelligence he could believe that. He left.

Seven

Warren swore. An army marched on its stomach; the police hobbled on its paperwork. If officers spent time at work instead of at their desks competing with forms, the crime statistics would go down without their having to be massaged by government fiddlers.

Chappell stepped past the half-open door. 'Sarge, I'm just—'

'Making a bloody nuisance of yourself. What d'you want?'

'I'm back from having a chat with Perce Swift. Says he knows nothing about the Querry job and started off telling me he and Edna ... It's odd, isn't it? I'd have expected Perce to shack up with someone who walks around in a dressing gown and has curlers in her hair, but she's not like that.'

'That's your report? His woman isn't like you're used to?'

'He said he'd not handled a job since he was last inside because Edna would clear off if he did. He'd been at home all night and Edna would swear to that. I persuaded him to try another story and then it seemed he was out boozing, but couldn't remember who with or when he returned home.

'I said he'd better come along here and make an official statement and that got him desperate because it would have made Edna think he was back on the job – I'm surprised that would surprise her ... Anyway, he offered some sharp information if I'd let him be.'

Warren began to sneeze.

'Caught a cold?'

'Hay fever, if it's any business of yours,' he snapped, between sneezes.

'Try tincture of comfrey. A friend of mine—'

'To hell with your friends.'

Chappell raised an eyebrow, then continued. 'Perce said what the information was. Damn near thumped him for trying to take the piss out of us.'

'What was it?'

'Information is being sold.'

Warren sneezed. 'Nothing new about that. Happens all the time and mostly it's crap.'

'The information made Querry Brade an easy job if carried out *before* the advanced security was installed.'

Warren silently swore.

'And the information is said to have come from here.'

'How did you react?'

'Haven't I said? Told him to stuff the sodding insult where it hurt the most. Given the chance, I'd have shown him what I meant.'

'Then it's as well you weren't. OK. Make certain you keep the information to yourself.'

'How d'you mean?'

'Start repeating that nonsense and it's likely someone in uniform with a bitch against CID will start wondering out loud if there could be some truth in the story.'

'If anyone starts that—'

'I know. You'll persuade him to shut up. Just keep your hands to yourself and your tongue still. Now clear off and leave me to work.'

Warren watched Chappell leave. As the door shut, he stared at the far wall. Until now, he had scorned the detective inspector's interpretation of events. Yet now . . . He tried to negate the new evidence. Yet immediately there was the question, how could Swift have known about the intended updating of the security without knowledge of Gregg's report? How feasible was it to claim coincidence was responsible for the theft's taking place after the survey, but before any improvements had been made?

He made his way along to the DI's room.

'Yes?'

He stood in front of the desk as Horton continued to write.

'Are you a mute messenger?'

'Didn't want to interrupt you, sir.'

Horton put down the pencil, settled back in the chair. 'You now have my undivided attention.'

'Chappell has just reported back. Swift first claimed he was in bed all night, then that he was on the booze, but can't remember who with. Swears he's been going straight because of Edna. Chappell used a little verbal pressure and Perce came out with the news that the robbery at Querry Brade had been so successful because the villains had inside information.'

'Shit!'

'It gets worse.'

'Well?'

'They bought the information from here.'

Horton spoke slowly. 'I've been trying my damnedest to prove all my assumptions wrong. I was seeing connections which weren't connected, refusing coincidences without accepting that coincidences do happen.'

Warren was surprised by the emotion with which Horton had spoken.

'What was your judgment on Chappell's reaction to what he was told?'

'Swift was trying to make us look crook.'

'He gave you no hint he was wondering if there could be a grain of truth in the story?'

'Quite the opposite.'

'How did you respond? '

'Agreed it was vicious nonsense; told him not to speak about it because it might start uniform tongues wagging.'

'Will he keep quiet?'

'He'll try, but may find that difficult.'

'One has to be prepared for word to get around?'

'He's a good copper but not the quietest.'

Horton tapped on the desk with the fingers of his right hand. 'How long has Gregg been security officer?'

'Since Pollock left to join another force up north and that must be some eighteen months back.'

'Draw up one list of every property Gregg has surveyed in that time and another of robberies from those properties.' Horton's fingers stilled.

'I still find it . . .'

'Difficult to believe one of us may be a traitor? That's why I can still hope you find nothing. Make certain no one gets the slightest hint of what you're doing or why.'

Warren left, glad he was not in command. Horton would not only be concerned that there might be a traitor in CID, but also that his career might be affected. He was at risk of being held guilty of a negligent command.

Eight

The shop had recently been sold to Joseph Chubb and he, in short time, revived both the store and the services offered. No longer did the show window display consist of an ancient safe and some hardly legible advertisements; now there was one modern, very strong safe and many security devices for the home and office.

Gregg entered, introduced himself and asked to speak to Mr Chubb. (A genuine name or one chosen to promote confidence?) He was shown into a small, newly decorated and comfortably furnished office.

Chubb, round-faced, plump, a ready smiler, came around the partner's desk and warmly shook hands. As security officer, Gregg was in a position to steer work his way. 'Good to see you again. I hope all's well with you?'

'Fine, thanks.'

'Glad to hear that. Sit you down and tell me how I can help – always presuming that's why you're here. But before that, would you like tea or coffee?'

He had drunk coffee here once before. 'Tea would be great.'

'Excuse me a moment.' Chubb walked past Gregg's chair and went out of the room, returned a moment later. He settled behind the desk. 'So what brings you here this time?'

'You'll have heard about the burglary at Querry Brade, just outside Lower Rington?'

'Indeed. The elderly couple must have been severely shocked. It is truly appalling the way in which crime and brutality have become part of normal life. I blame the video games. When my son reached the age of wanting them, I refused to allow him to play ones which were too violent.'

'It's a pity more don't do the same.'

'People tell you there's no connection between those games and modern thuggery; does advertising not affect buying? Do you have a son?'

'He's on his way.'

'Then you have much to learn!'

'I've no doubt on that score.'

'May I give you a brief word of advice?'

'Of course.'

'Never deny him something on the grounds that you didn't or couldn't have it when you were young. Do that and you'll be told with withering scorn that you belong to the Stone Age.'

'It sounds as if you know that from personal experience.'

'Indeed.'

'About the robbery. The wall safe in Querry Brade is a Safetight. Did you install it?'

'Memory tells me we were asked to remove an old safe in very poor condition – a penknife might, in skilled hands, have opened it – and to install a modern one. But if it is important, I had better check my files.'

'If you would be kind enough.'

Chubb used the intercom to ask his secretary to check the records. As he pushed the switch up to close the connection, there was a knock on the door and a middle-aged woman entered, crossed to the desk and put a tray down. 'There's some chocolate digestives for you, Mr Chubb.'

'Thank you, Mrs Arnold.'

She left.

'Milk?' Chubb asked.

'Yes, please.'

'First or last?'

'As it comes. Doesn't make any difference to the taste,' Gregg answered.

'Words to shock the connoisseur!' Chubb chuckled. 'I have a friend who refuses to drink if the milk is put in first.' He poured tea into two cups, added milk. 'Sugar?'

'A small spoonful, please.'

About to carry cup and saucer and biscuits across, Gregg forestalled Chubb and went up to the desk.

'Do help yourself to biscuits.'

Old-fashioned courtesy. And, as Chubb's son would no doubt add, from an old-fashioned father.

The intercom buzzed. The secretary expressed her apologies for the delay, but she had had to search through many old records. The firm had replaced an existing safe at Querry Brade seven years before and installed a Safetight 30 because that was what had been called for.

Chubb thanked her. He chuckled. 'My memory is not quite as distressed as my wife sometimes tries to make out!'

'Is Safetight a solid make?'

'Good, but arguably not the best. Occasionally we're asked to open one of their wall safes – naturally for legal reasons! – and we can be certain it will be quite a tough task.'

'The peterman at Querry Brade didn't have much trouble.'

'Then he's an expert. The papers talked about jewellery worth more than a million pounds. Is that an accurate figure?'

'I haven't seen an official figure, but it's probably about right and not the usual exaggeration.'

'Then with such valuable jewellery, the owner should not have relied on a small wall safe. There just isn't the space to build in sufficient defence.'

'The whole security of the house was poor. It was a robbery waiting to happen.'

'People seldom realize that money has to be defended with money.'

'There's one aspect of the robbery which worries us.'

'Which is?'

'The strong indication that the robbers knew exactly where the safe was.'

'I see. So now you want to know how reliable that indication is.' Chubb's manner had become less genial. 'To put it more bluntly, could one of my employees who installed the new safe have sold the information of its whereabouts? I met this question last year about another robbery and I'll give you the same answer as then. I don't employ anyone whose honesty can be impugned in any way.'

'Then it was probably luck which took the robbers to the right room and the right place in that room.'

'Or common sense. I read the safe was hidden behind a painting.'

'A framed print, to be exact.'

'Which is where a crook will look because he knows eight out of ten wall safes are stupidly positioned.'

'There was a line of four prints. He went straight to the far end one and swung it back.'

'He had to start somewhere. I'll speak plainly. It annoys me when someone comes here and assumes that one of my lads is a crook.'

'There has to be the possibility—'

'As there has to be the possibility that one of you is.'

About to answer angrily, Gregg checked the words. After a moment, he said, 'I accept your point. There is one more question. Have you any idea who installed the original safe?'

'You're now thinking one of them had a loose tongue?'

'We have to pursue every possibility.'

'Some of which are impossible.'

'Do you know who it was?'

'The firm from whom I bought the business? Mobyte Company.'

'Can you give me the name of someone who was in the firm?'

'The man who signed the contract of sale.'

'I'd be grateful if you'd let me have that.'

'It will need more delving into the records. Perhaps it will be best if I get back to you after I have uncovered the name.'

As Gregg drew into the side of the road, he decided he must have been given the wrong address. The ragstone two-up two-down was small and boxy and seemed unlikely to be the home of a top peterman who earned good money.

He left the car, opened the wooden gate which was in need of repair, knocked on the front door. The door was opened by Gutteridge – small, a weak face, an inability to stare anyone in the face, fingers of magic.

'You're the law, ain't you?' Gutteridge muttered.

'DC Gregg, county CID. I was told you lived here, but couldn't believe it. The top peterman in the county, maybe the country, living in the middle of a field with cows and sheep for company!'

'I like it.'

'Chilling out until it's time to start work again?'

'It ain't like that.'

'Never is.'

There was a brief silence.

'Mind if I come in?' Gregg asked.

Gutteridge moved to one side and he stepped into a small, sparsely furnished but dust-free room.

'You want . . . you want something, Mr Gregg?'

'You don't need an answer to that. You will have been expecting us around for the best part of two days.'

'Don't know what you're on about.'

'Sunday morning.'

'Still don't mean nothing.'

'The big robbery at Querry Brade.'

'That!'

'That.'

'I've maybe read or seen something about it.'

'Were the details correct?'

'How would I know?' Gutteridge's voice was now shrill.

'The safe was punched so neatly it was skill at its best. So my guv'nor said to come here and have a word with you before you had the chance to take off and enjoy life abroad.'

'That wasn't nothing to do with me. I'm going straight.'

'And I can walk on water.'

'Not touched a job in years.'

'Been living on your savings?'

'I'm working.'

'That's what I've been saying.'

'On a farm.'

'That's so absurd, I almost believe it.'

'When I was last inside, my old woman left me for someone else. Got thinking that with me inside, she'd been on her own and there was never any money because the fences don't play fair, only giving a pinch of what the stuff's worth, and I like spending what I've got. So she had to work stacking in a supermarket and that wasn't no life for her and wasn't no life for me. I was brought up on a farm. Did you know that, Mr Gregg?'

'It's not in your records.'

'Dad was brilliant with sheep. Used to help him and got to know something about it. Looked for a job on a farm what carried sheep and didn't get nowhere. Thought of going back to . . . Then Mr Whelan said he'd take me on and see if I was worth the hiring.'

'I'm tempted to cry hallelujah.'

Gutteridge looked at Gregg, then hastily away. 'Reckon a bloke don't ever change, don't you?' he said with weak aggression.

'That's the usual course of events, but they say it does happen.'

'Swear on my dad's grave I didn't touch that job.'

'You know the form so I'll believe you when you convince me you were somewhere a long way away, like the Outer Hebrides.'

'Ask Mr Whelan.'

'He owns this farm?'

'That's right.'

'He'll confirm you were here at midnight on Saturday?'

'I was at the party for him and his missus. Their silver wedding anniversary.'

'Where does he live?'

'Down the road in the farmhouse on the right; can't miss it on account of the oast house. He'll tell you I was with them.'

'Strangely, I'm hoping he'll confirm every word.'

Gutteridge's surprise was evident.

Gregg had crossed to the outside door and begun to open it when a call stopped him.

'Mr Gregg . . .'

He turned around.

'Do me a favour?' Gutteridge asked, his tone pleading.

'What and how?'

'Don't let on why you're asking. I told Mr Whelan I'd been working in a factory up north, so if he learns I've been inside, he'll maybe throw me off the farm.'

'I'll do the best I can. You have a car?'

'Yes, but . . .'

'Its number?'

'I don't understand why you're asking . . .'

'You don't have to do anything but give me the number and trust I'm not running you in for doing a hundred and twenty in a thirty limit.'

Nine minutes later, Gregg knocked on the door of a typical farmhouse with peg-tile roof which sloped down to within six feet of the ground to cover what had once been the outshut.

The door was opened by a middle-aged woman who wore an apron over a cotton frock. He introduced himself.

'The old man's out in the fields, lookering the sheep.' Her speech was soft and was touched by the local accent.

'Do you think he'll be long?'

'No knowing. There's an old ewe which forever finds holes in the fencing. He has to find her and then mend the hole.'

'I wonder if you can help me, to save bothering him? There was a hit-and-run near Manchester last Saturday, around midnight; a young woman was badly injured. Her companion took the number of the car, but he had been drinking and admitted he might have got it wrong. The owner of the car, whose number the man gave, is Mr Gutteridge. I've just had a word with him and he strongly denies he was anywhere near Manchester that night. Says he was at a party here. Can you confirm that?'

'I certainly can. It was Dad's and my silver wedding and we had friends along. Dad said we ought to ask Joe, who's a nice hard-working lad – not that he's a lad by many years – and he was with us until the party ended.'

'Was that before midnight?'

'More like two in the morning.' She chuckled. 'And I'll tell you who had to do the morning work – me, since I hardly drink.'

'Then obviously the witness did get the last two figures, five and nine, muddled and we'll have to try to work out what the number really was. Many thanks for your help, Mrs Whelan.'

'Have you heard how the poor woman is?'

'I'm afraid not.'

'Hope it's nothing too awful. A friend of mine was injured in a road accident and she's never been the same since.'

He said goodbye and walked to his car. Perhaps he should have said the injured woman had made a complete recovery to save Mrs Whelan's concern, but that would have been difficult since he had said she was badly injured only days before . . .

Warren listened to Gregg's report. 'So the next thing is to find out who was the bloke who installed the first safe and have a talk with him. You haven't done that?'

'Only just back from questioning Gutteridge.'

'When I started, we worked to the end, not to the clock.'

'And you were called a peeler.'

'Bloody humorous.' Warren scratched the back of his neck, which irritated, following a haircut. 'I'd have bet half my pension that he was the peterman. Not thought maybe he was pulling the wool over your eyes?'

'You'll not find anyone more genuine than Mrs Whelan and she was very definite saying he was with them well after midnight.'

'So we're not getting anywhere in either case.'

'How's that?'

'Nothing,' Warren snapped, annoyed at himself for having intimated the robbery was not their only pressing problem.

Nine

The English weather was at its most erratic. Dawn on Tuesday morning provided an almost cloudless sky; by eight the rain was light but threatening to become heavy. As Gregg drew up outside Hillview – a large, Regency-style house – the threat had become fact.

He hurried across the drive and into the dry of the large, ostentatious, out-of-character porch. He rang the bell and very quickly the door was opened by a woman with heavily made-up features and bouffant hair, dressed in a tight blouse and short skirt. If she walked down certain of the streets in town, he thought, she would constantly arouse misapprehensions. He gave his name and rank.

Her expression suggested sharp concern. Wondering which of her sins or peccadilloes had been uncovered? Policemen learned that if only totally honest people went to heaven, it must be sparsely occupied. 'I'd like a word with your husband, Mrs Cameron. It's purely routine,' he added to prevent her reaching deeper into memory.

'He's at work.'

'Where would that be?'

'I think he's in Lyons today.' She noted his expression. 'Because of his job, he has to go abroad a lot.'

'Do you know when he'll be returning?'

'It's supposed to be on Friday, but quite often he has to stay somewhere much longer than expected to sort out a problem. He's always saying that some executives have as much common sense as a dead duck. Can you tell me what you want to speak to him about?'

'We understand he worked for the Mobyte Company and

we're hoping he'll be able to tell us something concerning that firm.'

'You know he was only with them for a short time?'

'No, I didn't.'

'He was asked to shake some life into the firm. After a couple of months he gave the board his review of what needed to be done – that was something like selling some of the stores, modernizing those which were kept, retraining the staff. The board accepted his recommendations and a start was made on carrying them out; then they said they weren't going to continue, at least for a while, because of the cost involved. My husband decided the firm never would reach its potential with the existing board in power and he resigned. It was after that he set up on his own.

'As a matter of fact, I helped him at work for some of the time with Mobyte because one of his office staff was terminally ill, poor woman, and another had some sort of accident, can't remember what. So it's possible I might be able to answer your questions.'

'That would be very helpful.'

'Then come on inside, out of this beastly weather. I expect Tim will phone me tonight and tell me he had a cloud-free day and a wonderful dinner. As you know, Lyons is the home of the best French cooking.'

He did not know that.

They sat in a square sitting room, for his taste grossly over-furnished. The two paintings on one wall, ablaze with smudges of colour but no context, made him wonder if the modern artist ever knew what he was doing.

'What is it you want to know about Mobyte?' she asked.

'There's a store in Trentford – it's now in private hands – which was owned by them. Did you ever have anything to do with that?'

'I don't remember having done so. You want to know something peculiar to that store?'

'In one sense, yes.' He hastened to make himself clearer. 'It's a question of how thoroughly the backgrounds of the staff would have been checked before they were employed and if there was at any time a question about an individual's trustworthiness?'

'I can answer that without knowing the particular store. The honesty of any employee in the firm had to be beyond doubt. Indeed, my husband said it was the only breath of efficiency that wafted around the firm. The slightest question mark and the person would not be employed; if employed, any malfeasance meant dismissal. Is that of any help?'

'Yes, it is.'

'When my husband rings me, would you like me to ask him to get in touch with you so he can give you more information?'

'Since that would be only to confirm what you have just told me, I'm sure there's no need to trouble him.'

Warren was seated behind his desk. 'You reckon it's safe to accept what Mrs Cameron told you?'

'I do, yes.'

'When is the husband returning?'

'Officially, on Friday, but he's quite often held back by work. Since he's in Lyons, I imagine he'll be at least one day late.'

'Why?'

'That's where you enjoy the best cooking in France. Didn't you know that?'

'Not interested.'

'They probably add pâté de foie gras to everything . . .'

'Didn't you hear me say I'm not interested? Got better things to do than spend the day thinking about my stomach. What's his work?'

'From the sound of things, some sort of efficiency guru.'

'You didn't ask?'

'Didn't see the need to know.'

'You told her to tell him to get in touch with you when he gets back?'

'Said I didn't think that would be necessary.'

'Seems like an efficiency expert could do you some good.'

Warren picked up a sheet of paper, read what was on it, dropped it back on to the desk. 'A couple of hours ago, a keeper rang in to say one of 'em has found a burned-out car in Oak Wood. D'you know where that is?'

'Part of the Widcombe estate.'

'Owned by a very rich Member of Parliament who claims expenses for his groceries and more than a pound a mile for travelling in his car.'

'Resourceful gentleman.'

'There hasn't been a gentleman in Parliament for the last fifty years . . . Obviously, there's the possibility the car was used in the Querry Brade job.'

'Then the keepers haven't been doing much of a job if it's been there nearly a week and they've only just come across it.'

'See what you make of things.'

'Sarge, I was hoping—'

'You aren't paid to hope.'

Gregg left. Warren's present mood reflected his home life. His son had been arrested for vandalism three weeks ago.

The rain slowly eased as Gregg drove the five miles to the Widcombe estate. Passing the elaborate gateway to his left, he had a quick glimpse of the 200-yard long drive and the eastern end of Widcombe Manor – not, as might be expected, an Elizabethan or Jacobean gem, but a characterless, sprawling Edwardian pile.

On the right-hand side of the road, set back, was a brick bungalow. Judging this to be the home of an estate employee, he stopped the car, walked up the short path, knocked on the front door. A middle-aged, sallow-faced woman answered.

'Detective Constable Gregg. We had a call that a burned-out car has been found in the woods and I've come to have a look at it.'

'It's my Bert phoned. The other side of Oak Wood.' A wave of the hand indicated the trees a hundred yards back from the cottage.

'Can you tell me where to find it?'

'See that ride there?'

It was difficult to distinguish the small gap in the trees.

'That leads to the other side and the clearing where the car is.'

'Thanks.'

'You ain't going dressed like that?'

He smiled. 'I've got my rough gear in the car.'

He returned to the car, put on wellingtons and a plastic mackintosh, walked across the field to the accompaniment of clapping wings as several pigeons flew away. The ride was barely muddy, despite the rain; on either side was a typical muddle of oak, ash, chestnut and hornbeam trees, clumps of rhododendron bushes, bracken and bramble undergrowth. A squirrel appeared ahead of him and with raised tail raced along the path for a few yards, then swerved right and climbed an oak; from a safe height, it peered around the trunk to watch him pass. Young pheasants, cautious yet not afraid of him, being still hand fed, scratched their way hither and thither.

The blackened shell of the car was in a small clearing, close to the edge of the wood. A careful search around it disclosed nothing of any consequence.

'Are you from the police?'

He was startled, not having heard the approach of the stocky man with a weather-beaten face, who carried a broken gun over his left arm. 'Detective Constable Gregg. You are?'

'Bert Ankley, head keeper.'

Following good PR practice, Gregg thanked him for informing the police. 'Can you say how long it's been here?'

'Wasn't when Jim made his last round of the beat.'

'Which would have been last night?'

'That's right.'

'At what time?'

'Poacher-time. As it was getting dark.'

'Jim is what?'

'Second under-keeper. Solid lad in spite of his missus always complaining about him working all hours.'

The men who had invaded Querry Brade would not have waited days before getting rid of the car used in that robbery, so this one had taken no part in it. But since there was every probability this was not just someone getting rid of a clapped-out old banger, that it was connected with some other criminal activity, after noting down the registration number, he began to check what was left of the interior.

Gregg parked, crossed the pavement, entered home. He called out. Wendy stepped out on to the upstairs landing.

'You're back rather late.'

'Life is one long rush.'

'I was having a rest in bed and fell fast asleep.' She started to come down the stairs.

'Have you been feeling rotten?'

'Just lazy.'

The truth, or said to belie his worries?

She reached the floor, kissed him, linked her arm with his. 'Come on in here. I want to say something.'

They entered the sitting room, after having to separate, and settled on the settee.

He spoke lightly. 'I gather you have an important announcement to make. Has a lady called here to say we've won a million pounds on the Premium Bonds, but she needed to be certain we are the people we're supposed to be? If so, we'll buy a seventeenth-century timber-framed cottage and that dining table you saw, made from one piece of wood . . .'

'On Sunday, I behaved like a harridan.'

'You're far too young to do that.'

'I should never have gone for you as I did.'

'And I should have had a better memory.'

'It was silly of me to expect you to remember.' She leaned against him, took his left hand in hers. 'Forgive?'

'I've such a terrible memory, I've forgotten what it is I am to forgive.'

'I have a wonderful husband.'

'There are some things on which we will never disagree.'

'But that doesn't mean you're perfect.'

'Now you're being less than factual.'

'Guinevere rang earlier.'

'No wonder you needed a long rest.'

'We're invited to supper tomorrow.'

'Surely it's to dinner, not supper?'

'I was forgetting.'

'White tie?'

'Not this time.'

'You thought up a previous engagement?'

'Of course not.'

'Then did you suggest a simple meal since we never eat much at night – just a boiled egg and salad. Even she would have difficulty ruining that.'

'She's going to prepare a special meal for us.'

'We must make certain to have stomach pills with us.'

'You're being rather unkind.'

'A man who faces unpleasant facts . . . Poor Sidney. He used to consider himself something of a gourmet.'

'That must be a long time ago.'

'Obviously, before he married.'

'How is he?'

'Looking very down.'

'Is there trouble at work?'

'Much more likely the trouble's at home. Perhaps Gwen has had a very long-lasting headache.'

'There are times when you have a one-track mind.'

'Thinking of her, that's inevitable.'

'You've said she doesn't appeal to you.'

'There's a difference between sex appeal and sex appreciation . . . I'm going to have a drink.'

'Now you've suggested it, so will I.'

'One small sherry.'

'Then you will have only half a tin of lager.'

'Are you still demanding pregnant inequality?'

Ten

At ten fifteen on Wednesday, Vehicles reported that the burned-out car in Oak Wood had been stolen in East London three days previously; there was reason to believe it had been used in a smash-and-grab raid.

Gregg spent much of the morning investigating the loss of three small statues from a Trentford garden; had this not belonged to the mayor, the case would have been left to Uniform. Shown photographs of the statues, Gregg decided it was quite possible that the mayor was kinky.

At half past four in the afternoon, he met Tynam in the reading room of the public library. Tynam, an informer who suffered from severe halitosis, had named the library as the meeting place because had he been seen in the company of a detective, his life expectancy would have sharply shortened, but those he feared were unlikely to be anywhere near any centre of learning.

They sat at the small central table on which were current magazines and newspapers; behind them were locked, glass-fronted bookshelves in which were luxuriously produced art books.

'There's a buzz on, Mr Gregg,' Tynam said.

'Which says what?' Gregg moved back a little to try to avoid the next exhalation of laden breath.

'A name for the big job.'

'You're talking about Querry Brade?'

'It's called something like that.'

'Who's in the frame?'

'There ain't many sharp enough to work as slick as he

did. Calls for experience. Kids want everything today, not tomorrow, so there ain't many of his mark still around. When I was a nipper, one worked first, spent later. You wanted to buy something on tick, you had to put down part of the price . . .'

Gregg nodded from time to time to suggest he was listening. Tynam seemed to consider himself a political commentator. But he was a useful informer, registered in the book which named his kind, the money he was paid, and the practical result of the information given, to provide a defence against any accusation that an officer had been working with the informer rather than using him.

A stern-looking woman, one of the staff, was regarding them through the glass half of the door. Gregg, amused, decided that unless she knew who he was, she was coming to a spinsterly judgement concerning the relationship between the two of them.

Tynam finally stopped talking.

'Couldn't put it more neatly myself. Now, name.'

'What's it worth?'

'The usual.'

'You'll see the insurance company knows it was me?'

'Yes.'

'Could be big reward money, couldn't it?'

'If all the jewellery is recovered.'

'You will tell them it was me gave you the name?'

'Rest easy. You ought to know police officers aren't allowed to share in rewards.'

'Then there ain't no need to worry.'

'Your faith in me is rewarding.'

Tynam hesitated, then said in little more than a whisper, 'Joe Gutteridge.'

'Sorry, that's a no-no. Joe was at an anniversary party when the job was on.'

'You believe that?'

'Why not?'

'Because he'd lie his way out of hell.'

'He has a concrete alibi.'

'I'm telling you—' he began excitedly.

'Calm it or you'll convince the lady outside that the worst is about to happen. Accept Joe is crystal clear, so your dreams of riches have to wait.'

Tynam began to chew his lower lip. Gregg moved his chair back, preparing to stand. 'Best hope the next time you'll be on target.'

'There's something more, Mr Gregg.'

'Then let's have it.'

'Don't want no one else to hear it . . .'

'Since we're the only ones in here, no one will.'

Tynam spoke in a very low voice. At the beginning, Gregg could not make out all the words, but he understood enough to lean forward and brave the stench in order to hear what was being said.

Gregg entered Warren's room.

'Ever thought of knocking?' Warren demanded angrily as he folded up several sheets of paper.

'I thought as the door was open . . .'

'It wasn't meant to be.'

'Then maybe I didn't mean to come in.'

'Get any smarter and you'll be on night duty for the next month.'

'I'm back from talking to one of my snouts, Sarge.'

'Is it entered in the book?'

'I need a word before making the entry.'

'Why?'

'He gave me the name of the peterman who did the Querry Brade job.'

'Who was it?'

'Joe Gutteridge.'

'Useless. You ought to bloody well know that.'

'I told him so. His misery was so great, he added something more. It's all a complete load of cod's—'

'Then you don't have to be told to forget it.'

'But do I write it in the book?'

'I'm so stressed I've a heart attack sitting on my shoulder

and the last thing I need is you coming in here and waffling on about nothing.'

'He claims someone in the force is selling information which is why the Querry Brade job was so successful.'

Warren tried to conceal his reaction to what was said. 'You listened?'

'I said, it's crap. There's no one in our outfit would touch that sort of thing.'

'Then there's the end of it.'

'But do I enter it in the book as information given to me by the snout?'

'Not unless you want the guv'nor cursing you to hell. One more thing. Keep that absurd lie to yourself.'

'Wasn't intending to do anything else, Sarge.'

The Lodges lived half a mile from the Greggs, in a house one bedroom larger yet which from the road looked similar. Inside, there could hardly have been a greater contrast. Guinevere had read that bright colours were the *dernier cri*. 'Too many purple patches,' Gregg had said after their first visit.

Conversation had been general and brisk and the first round of drinks had been enjoyed, when Lodge said, 'Have you been up to something, Andy?'

'Lots of things, all enjoyable and therefore illegal,' Gregg replied. 'Why ask?'

'I needed a word with the skipper, but couldn't find him until someone said try the catacomb. He was there, working at the table. Thought he must have had to do something he couldn't palm on to one of us. Made me wonder what. Tried to get a look at the opened file, but he realized what was going on and in a hell of a temper, slammed it shut and said if I'd nothing better to do, he'd find me something. Reminded me of the time I read one of my dad's letters – don't know why, it wasn't interesting – and he caught me at it. Landed me a fourpenny one. Never read another person's letter since. Funny, really. People shout that to smack a child is an assault which will affect him for life, yet one good slap on the bum is a certain cure and no physical or mental harm done.'

'Not so certain about mental harm in your case. But what's all that to do with anything?'

'It was your security file.'

'So?'

'Why was he reading it in the catacomb and not his office? And why so eager to stop me seeing what he was doing?'

'Reluctant to be seen with adult fiction.'

'Has he given you a hint of something wrong?'

'What d'you mean?'

'Maybe one of your surveys has burped?'

'The only problem I meet is persuading people to pay for the work I recommend. Suggest someone spends a thousand to protect a couple of hundred thousand pounds' worth of gear and he hums and haws.'

'There's been nothing unusual going on?'

'What do you call unusual in our job?'

Guinevere spoke sharply. 'For heaven's sake, do you have to talk business now?'

'I was just—' Lodge began.

'Being very boring.'

'Sorry, but I never was a witty before-dinner speaker.'

'Or a good host. All our glasses have been empty for ages.'

Lodge stood, did not immediately move. 'All I was wondering was if the sarge had said anything . . .'

'Didn't you hear me telling you to shut up?' she snapped.

'I hear and obey, sweet mistress mine.' He collected the glasses, walked through to the kitchen.

'I must make certain the meal's coming along all right,' Guinevere said. 'It's an experiment and I'm a little worried it won't come out as it should.'

'There can't be any doubt on that score since you've done the cooking,' Gregg said. He received a surreptitious kick on the ankle from Wendy.

'There was an article in a magazine saying Spanish

cooking was all the rage this year. I decided to try one of the recipes they gave.'

'Was it in Spanish?'

'Of course not! Then I wouldn't know what to do.'

Wendy kicked Gregg's ankle a second time before he could make another ambiguous comment.

'It said to use cream with the steak. That seemed so odd it had to be wrong and I left it out. But I did everything else, like beating the meat. I've never done that before.'

'You surprise me.'

'Stop it,' Wendy muttered angrily.

Lodge returned with refilled glasses.

They drove away.

'It wasn't quite as grim as I expected,' Wendy said.

'Then your expectations must have been low.' Gregg turned the corner. 'I reckon the meat must have come off one of the bulls killed in a corrida last year.'

'I was talking about the whole evening. And you ought to be ashamed of yourself for some of the things you said.'

'She'll have enjoyed the double meanings.'

'That doesn't make your rudeness any the less.'

He braked to a stop at traffic lights.

'What was Sidney going on about?' she asked.

'With reference to what?'

'When he mentioned speaking to Sergeant Warren in the . . . What did he call it?'

'The catacomb.'

'Why that?'

'It's the part of the basement where all long-hold records are stored. A forest of dead, unnecessary paperwork created by impossible targets being set and demands for explanations when they haven't been met.'

'I thought he seemed worried about what the sergeant was doing there. He kept on asking you questions, even after Guinevere had told him to stop talking shop.'

'He's got an active curiosity.'

'Why should Warren have been studying your file?'

'A dozen and one possible reasons. He'll have been checking up on something.'

'You aren't in any trouble, are you?'

'What on earth makes you ask that?'

'I don't know. It's just there seemed something odd about the way Sidney was so persistent after she'd told him to stop. And he sounded odd when he asked you whether Warren had said anything.'

'In what way odd?'

'Kind of . . . not really excited, but excitedly worried.'

'Sounds a bit complicated.'

'I suppose it's imagination. But something else wasn't. Did you notice what she was wearing?'

'A black chiffon blouse with bishop sleeves, decorated with paste clusters.'

'Couldn't be less accurate, but what's happened to make you describe women's clothes as if you knew something about the subject?'

'The last time I had my hair cut, I had to wait so I picked up a women's magazine. There was a full-page photo of a woman in a dress which only cost fifteen hundred pounds. That "only" intrigued me.' The lights changed and he drove forward. 'How rich does one have to be that fifteen hundred for a bit of material becomes "only"?'

'Impossible to explain to a man who thinks nothing of wearing socks of different colours . . . Anyway, I wasn't referring to her frock, but her brooch.'

'On her tit.'

'Breast.'

He chuckled.

In Sandy Lane, the parking space in front of their house had been taken by their neighbour. Gregg drove on another twenty-five yards to appropriate someone else's space. He yawned as he switched off the engine.

'Very tired?' she asked.

'It's not going to take me long to fall asleep.'

He was wrong. In bed, for once he did not read as she

did and after a while, he said, 'Not putting your light out before dawn?'

'Just finishing the chapter.'

His mind was beginning to drift when she shut her book and put it down on the bedside table. She switched off the light, snuggled into a comfortable position. He reached across to touch her side as a last goodnight gesture, withdrew his hand.

'Did you look carefully at it?' she asked.

'What?'

'Her brooch.'

'No.'

'It's odd.'

Greater love hath no man than this, that a man listen to his wife when he longs to sleep. 'What is?'

'Some time back I was walking along East Street and stopped to look in the window of the jeweller's.'

'To see if the scarab ring was still there?'

'No,' she answered sharply.

One little white lie, he thought.

'It was just shopping curiosity. In the centre of the window display was a brooch in the shape of a bat flying across a crescent moon which was set on a black-velvet-covered display stand. It was Victorian, in gold, silver, and diamonds, designed by some name I've forgotten.'

'And it stirred your desire?'

'I'm not certain I even liked the piece.'

'A trifle too batty?'

'I suppose you couldn't resist that. I was very surprised to see Guinevere wearing it.'

'Why shouldn't she have liked it even if you didn't?'

'It cost two thousand pounds.'

'Then what she was wearing on her . . . *breast* was a copy.'

'No. It was the real thing.'

'People have become very clever at simulating.'

'I tell you, those diamonds on her brooch were real.'

'If you say so.'

'Couldn't you see them flash colours when she moved?'
'Didn't look.'

'You expect me to believe that when her dress was so tight? It's typical of her to keep complaining about how little money they have and then to spend recklessly. That brooch has to be way over the top.'

She said no more and soon she was breathing slowly. Despite his earlier sleepiness, he now began to wonder why Warren had been in the catacomb, reading his file.

Eleven

Warren entered Horton's room.

'Well?'

'I've just finished checking the two lists, sir. I'm afraid it's taken rather a long time, but working on my own ...'

'What's the result?'

'Not a single other incident of a survey being closely followed by a robbery. In fact, there's not even been one *some time* after a survey Gregg made.'

'Thank God!' He stared down at the top of the desk, his expression one of sharp relief.

'Gregg's reported a snout has told him information concerning the house was sold by the police.'

'That kind of rumour travels faster than the speed of sound. There isn't a villain who won't rush to believe that and hurry to tell his mates ... How did Gregg respond?'

'Told the snout it was a load of crap. I said to forget it and not enter anything about it in the book.'

'I suppose there has to be some point in trying to shut the stable door.' He looked back at Warren. 'Did you get any impression as to whether Gregg had wind of our suspicions?'

'There was no suggestion he had.'

'Let's hope that's right. Nothing more bitter than learning one's unjustly under suspicion of being a traitor. Equally bitter to know one is responsible for setting up that suspicion.'

'As you said, sir, we had to check up.'

'Duty doesn't always salve the guilty mind.'

'I can't see we're responsible.'

'Judge not, that ye be not judged.'

'If we don't judge, we're not doing our job.'

'A very practical attitude.'

Warren accepted that as criticism.

'With one problem out of the way, we're still left with another. Who carried out the job? The known local petermen have been questioned and for the moment seem to be clear. Do we question them again to find out if one has succeeded in foxing us?'

'There can't be much point in talking to Gutteridge again. His alibi is watertight.'

'Swift?'

'It would be a good idea to talk to him even if Chappell was convinced he wasn't involved. Chappell can be a bit slap-dash at times, but when it comes to character judgement, he's usually spot on. He's convinced Swift was telling the truth when he claimed he didn't have the bottle to team up with violence. But then, Swift's only corroboration is his wife who's as sharp as they come.'

'Send someone else along.'

'Gregg?'

'To ease our consciences?'

'Because he's as good as anyone.'

'What about you going along with him?'

'Two of us might overwhelm Swift. Panics easily.'

'When he's a top peterman?'

'Strange that. Call him timid and you're right. Yet he'll work a room when there are people sleeping on either side of that. If that were me, I'd be too nervous to do anything.'

'The downside of being an honest man. Have you asked other forces for news of top petermen who seem to have gone walkabout?'

'Yes, sir. Perhaps we'll get some answers in a month's time.'

'Ever the optimist! The second man was obviously chosen for back-up weight which makes it likely he's local. I imagine you're asking around for any gorilla who's spending freely?'

'Been doing that from the start. The superintendent was very unwilling, but I managed to persuade him to give us a PC to help.'

'What about the fences?'

'They're being questioned. Jewellers and pawn shops have been, or are being, asked to be on the lookout for someone offering good jewellery.'

'Am I right that there aren't any photos of the jewellery to distribute?'

'The Irwins never bothered to have any taken for themselves. The insurance company still hasn't provided them.'

'Presumably, Gregg advocated they should?'

'He stressed the need to do so, but nothing was done. There would just about have been time had the Irwins reacted sharply.'

'The more one has, the more careless one becomes. What about the insurance company – have you had a word with them regarding the reward?'

'They have agreed to increase after accepting Irwin's offer of a contribution, but are not yet ready to name an amount.'

'Have you been on to the PR man at county HQ to tell him to publicize the reward widely as soon as the amount is known?'

'Yes, sir.'

'Hurry the insurance people to come through with a figure. The sooner the news is out, the sooner anyone in the know will be judging the balance between the risk of talking with the reward for doing so. Have Forensics come through with anything?'

'Not so far.'

'I've had the chief super on the phone, asking what progress we're making. He was less than flattering when I told him.'

'We've been having to put so much of our effort into finding out whether or not Gregg had been selling information.'

'I could hardly put that forward as an excuse when it displays our lack of trust in our own team.'

'I refuse to believe Gregg could be crook.'

'You would like me to reword what I said? Display *my* lack of trust?'

Warren was too experienced to answer.

By the middle of the afternoon, the sun had returned and the air was warm. Gregg walked along East Street until he reached Mandy and Rill. He looked through the show window. On the velvet-covered stand there was now a diamond and emerald ring, priced at £7,500 – pocket money for some; unobtainable riches for him. Presumably, the bat brooch, which had concerned Wendy, had been sold – or removed from its prime position in the name of variety. Or was it now on Guinevere's breast? If so, Sidney had dug himself into a financial pit from which it would be all but impossible for him to escape. There was no fool like an ardent fool.

He entered the shop. A smartly dressed woman was talking to an assistant who held an opened jewellery case in his hand. Meredith, the owner of the shop, middle-aged and conventionally dressed in black coat and striped trousers, came through the doorway at the back of the second counter. 'Good afternoon. It's Detective Constable . . .?'

'Gregg.'

'Of course. Sorry about that lapse of memory. One of age's costs. How can I help you?'

'You'll know about the robbery at Querry Brade. They cleared out all the family jewellery, so I'm here asking the usual – to inform us if you suspect any of the pieces are being offered to you.'

'Of course. But I rather doubt that will happen. I hope we have the reputation of demanding good provenance before buying anything. You have photographs of the pieces?'

'Not yet. Only a detailed list.' He brought one of several paper-clipped pages out of the case he was carrying, handed it across.

Meredith visually skimmed through the first page, then

the second. 'If it is all of good quality, it provided a rich haul.'

'I was told it was top quality.'

He put the list down on the glass-topped counter. 'We'll keep our eyes wide open and get in touch immediately if there's cause.'

'Many thanks.' Gregg hesitated, said, 'For a long time, I've been meaning to ask what a scarab ring is . . .'

He raised a carefully groomed eyebrow. 'I fear I have only the most elementary knowledge on that subject. A genuine one was a gem, carved in Ancient Egypt, in the form of a scarab beetle – which, I have been told, covers a whole wide range of insects and includes the dung beetle. It was symbolic of resurrection and immortality so the rings were worn as amulets to ward off illness and all other evils.'

'Were husbands included in the other evils?'

Meredith dutifully smiled.

'Is there one in your window?'

'There has been for the last few months, since an elderly gentleman, who'd been living in Cairo, brought it in, wishing to sell. He said he believed it was genuine, but accepted it was not after I showed him the opinion of an expert. It was possibly tens of years old, not thousands. Scarab rings have been made again since the time of popular tourism.'

'May I see it?'

'Naturally.'

As Meredith moved away, Gregg stared down at the rings under the counter, his mind drifting. Wendy had denied she had stopped the other day to look at the scarab ring, but he was certain it had been that which had caught her attention, not diamonds, sapphires, rubies, emeralds, or pearls.

'This is it, Mr Gregg.'

He took the ring. A dark stone had been carved into the form of a beetle. Hanging from the gold ring was a price tag. He read it, was none the wiser because there were three letters, divided by a forward slash.

'Four hundred and fifty pounds,' Meredith said, answering the question which had not been asked.

Gregg thanked the other, left, walked back down East Street to High Street and towards the second jeweller in town. When he came abreast of the NatWest bank, he stopped. He had been secretly saving to meet any extra expenses after the birth of Charles (his preference; hers was Henry – agreement not yet reached). The present of a scarab ring would bring her the extra delight of a long-held desire fulfilled and take her mind off the fact that her birthday fell on a Friday the thirteenth. (She had always denied she was superstitious, yet a Friday the thirteenth had her waiting for disasters.) But how could he possibly justify a present which would all but empty his savings?

Just before closing time, Meredith handed Gregg the small, square jewel box, wrapped in gold-coloured paper. 'I hope it does its duty, Mr Gregg, and wards off all evil.'

'Me too!'

Gregg left, suffering the uneasy worry of someone who knew he had done something emotionally satisfying yet logically unjustifiable.

Twelve

Lodge watched their guests drive away in the BMW convertible. He shut the front door, locked it, returned to the sitting room. Guinevere was lying on the settee, careless that her frock had ridden up her thighs.

'Let's have another drink,' she said.

'It's after half eleven and . . .'

'Why are you always such a moaning misery?'

'Just a quick one, then. I have to be up smartly in the morning.'

'It was a very successful evening, wasn't it?'

'Yes.'

'Is that all you have to say after the trouble I've been to to make it successful?'

He could have added Phillip had talked about little other than how successful he was; Cynthia had name-dropped and as she drank her third glass of cava had expressed her judgement that cava could almost, not quite, provide a reasonable substitute for champagne; the leg of lamb had been overcooked, the beans undercooked . . .

'They're so amusing.'

That depended on one's sense of humour.

'You'd never guess her father has a title.'

'She does tend "accidentally" to let slip that fact.'

'How typical of you! You dislike anyone who has more than you. You're a Marxist.'

'Just a me-first-ist.'

'What a stupid thing to say. Are we going to have another drink?'

He went through to the kitchen. There was just enough

in the remaining bottle of Anna de Codorníu to refill her
flute.

'Aren't you having one?' she asked, as he handed her the
glass.

'I decided not.'

'To make me feel uneasy, I suppose.'

'To make certain I wake up when the alarm goes off.'

She drank, lowered the glass. 'Phillip starts work at seven
in the morning and often doesn't get back home until eight
or nine. That's a terribly long day.'

'I often work more hours than that.'

'And are a hell of a lot less successful.'

'Depends how you define success.'

'You know exactly what I mean.'

'The make of car one runs, the size of the house one
lives in, the holidays in far-off and exotic places?'

'God, you're sour . . . You heard they're off to Jamaica
soon?'

'Each of them kindly told me so – Phillip twice.'

'Cynthia said we must join them. Wasn't that very friendly
of her?'

'Safe.'

'What on earth do you mean by that?'

'Even on a package holiday, going there would cost a
bundle and you can be certain that's not how they intend
to travel.'

'How can you be certain?'

'Cynthia would be afraid of having to mix with the kind
of people who go on package holidays.'

'You're so jealous of them.'

'Not so, since I don't wear rose-tinted spectacles.'

'They're green ones.' She drank. When she next spoke,
her tone was softer. 'I'm sure it wouldn't be nearly as expensive as you're making out.'

'We decided on Torremolinos for our holiday.'

'You decided. Jamaica would be ten times nicer.'

'And twenty times more expensive.'

'It's always money with you.'

'Not surprising since I don't earn a couple of hundred thousand a year.'

'What a small mind you have.'

And a small pocket.

Because of Guinevere's earlier attitude, Lodge had expected that in bed her goodnight kiss would express indifference and she would immediately turn over, away from him. Her kiss proved to be generous and she lay facing him.

'I really would love to go to Jamaica,' she said.

'So would I. But it's just not on.'

'The bank would give us a loan.'

'Not a big enough one. It's so much more than just the flight. With them, it would be a five-star hotel, meals in expensive restaurants, shopping.'

'If the bank's so stingy, there are all those people advertising on television and offering up to twenty-five, fifty thousand pounds.'

'With the current situation, credit's drying up and in any case, it would mean a second mortgage. The one we have is more than enough for us.'

'You always find reasons for not enjoying life.'

'The finances do that.'

'It's such a pity you haven't got a job that pays a decent salary.'

'I would have hated any form of office job.'

'And what you want is all that matters?'

There was an obvious response to that. He did not deliver it.

She switched off her bedside light. He was about to do the same when she turned on to her side and moved close to him, her breasts against his arm. 'I've had a wonderful idea.'

She could raise fire more quickly than a professional arsonist. 'What is it?'

'You can't guess?' She undid the buttons of his pyjama jacket and lightly ran her hand down his chest; she raised one leg and laid it across him; she kissed him with apparent hunger.

He slid his hand under her nightdress.

'Please listen before we . . .' Her whisper ceased as if too embarrassed to speak the words. 'All you have to do is ask your aunt for the money.'

'What money?' His mind was not at its sharpest.

'That we'll need to go to Jamaica with Cynthia and Phillip.'

'I can't ask her for any more so soon after she was generous enough to allow me to buy your brooch.'

'You're her only nephew, you always get on so well with her. She'll want you to be happy.'

'You don't understand.'

'Don't I? You think I can't realize that all that matters as far as you're concerned is what you want? All right, then what you want doesn't count either.' She forced his hand away, removed her leg, turned on to her side.

Into his racing mind came the muddled memory of a quotation he had read, but forgotten until now. *I cannot endure the torture of lingering, aching passion.*

Thirteen

The alarm rang. Gregg awoke, stretched out to touch Wendy a good morning as he always did and found only space. He hurried out of bed, went out on to the landing and shouted her name.

'I'm downstairs,' came the distant reply.

She was on one of the easy chairs in the sitting room.

'What's the matter?' he asked worriedly, his mind lining up possible problems.

'I couldn't sleep and instead of waking you with my twisting and turning, I came down here.'

'Have you been sick?'

'Only the daily routine.'

'Why can't the doctors find something to stop it?'

'They did, with tragic results. Nature usually prefers to take its own course ... Do I get a good morning kiss?'

'A birthday one.' He bent down and kissed her; she briefly stroked his cheek before he stood upright. 'Before long you're going to have a squalling infant to deny you sleep.'

'And you'll have the pleasure of singing nursery rhymes to quieten him.'

'Nothing could be more guaranteed to do the opposite since I cannot sing in tune. Hang on here a moment.'

'I'm not going anywhere.'

He left, returned with the wrapped jewellery box. 'A small present, large with love.' He handed it to her.

She looked at it, then at him. She unwrapped the decorated paper, hesitated before lifting the lid of the box. 'Oh, my God!'

'If it doesn't fit snugly, it can be altered.'

She brought out the ring and slid it on to a finger. 'It doesn't need altering. It was obviously made for me. It's so wonderful . . . I feel as if I'm waltzing on a cloud.'

'Then avoid blue sky.'

'If only you knew how I feel.'

'I've a good idea.'

'I have the most wonderful husband.'

They sat at the small table in the corner of the kitchen. He had a full breakfast; she a bowl of cornflakes.

He ate the last piece of egg on toast, looked at his watch. 'I need to get a move on.'

'Andy . . .'

'Yes?'

'Did this wonderful ring come from Mandy and Rill?'

'It did.'

'The first time I saw it in the window, I hesitated . . . then couldn't resist going in and asking what it cost, even though I knew I couldn't afford it. Five hundred pounds.'

'Then it had been reduced, probably because it didn't sell quickly enough.'

'Reduced to what?'

'Not a question you are allowed to ask.'

'I've asked it.'

'Not a question I am going to answer.'

'It's so . . . I suppose people would say it's silly of me to hold it so emotionally valuable, but it . . . well, brings my parents a little closer and in focus. I know I'm not talking sense.'

'You're talking perfect sense. Sorry, but I must leave.'

'Please tell me one thing. Did it cost all our savings?'

'Not a penny has gone out of our Abbey National account.'

'Then how . . . how could you manage?'

'The day you told me you were pregnant, I decided to save on the quiet as much as I could in order to buy something that would tell you how proud I felt. Your ring was bought with silent savings.'

'But you give me most of your salary for housekeeping and the mortgage.'

'I forwent extras.'

'What extras?'

'A couple of pints with the lads after work, a full meal at the canteen . . . that sort of thing.'

'You've been starving yourself?'

'When you do the cooking?'

'You've always enjoyed a drink with the boys.'

'I've enjoyed buying the ring a thousand times more.'

'I . . . I don't know what to say.'

'You've already silently said it.'

'You're one of them, aren't you?' Edna said aggressively.

'I'm not certain how to answer that,' Gregg answered lightly.

'You're a copper. Come to accuse Perce of being busy because you lot can't believe a man can go straight.'

'We try, but it can be a little difficult. Is he here?'

'Why can't you leave him alone?'

'Because he has an interesting past.'

'He ain't worked since he came out last.'

'Then he's nothing to worry about.'

'Nothing? When you lot keep coming here, accusing him, calling him a liar, frightening him?'

'I'll try to do none of those things and just have a pleasant chat.'

'You act like you was the Gestapo.'

'I promise you I've left the thumbscrews back at the station.'

'Enjoy it, don't you? Making out how important you are . . .'

'Come on, give it a break. Where is he? Upstairs, downstairs, in his lady's chamber?'

'In the front room,' she answered sullenly.

'Inviting me in?'

'So as you can drag him off?'

'In style, on a tumbrel.'

She finally moved to allow him to enter. She slammed the door shut, pushed past him, called out, 'It's them come back, Perce,' went into the kitchen.

'Regular as the dust cart,' Swift said sourly.

'Good morning, Perce,' Gregg said as he entered.

'It was,' Swift muttered, as he moved away from the window, through which he had been looking. He slumped down on one of the chairs. The fluffy cat regarded Gregg with apparent dislike, jumped up on to Swift's lap and dabbed his hand with a paw, demanding to be stroked.

Gregg, surprised by the orderly state of the room – as Chappell had been – settled on the second easy chair. 'We're wondering what more you can tell us about the big job?'

'What big job?'

'Ignorance does not become you.'

'Like I told the other bloke, I was here all night.'

'That's what you first said. Then you corrected yourself and said you were on the booze.'

'She'll tell you I came back with me head floating.'

'Unfortunately, I have to remember wives tend to support their husbands and you said you'd entered quietly so as not to wake her.'

'Calling her a liar?'

'Loyal is the word.'

'I was on the booze.'

'Celebrating?'

'Why won't you believe me?'

'The job was so sharp, people are still talking about it in hushed tones. When there's talk, there are whispers.'

'What whispers?'

'About you.'

'What you saying?'

'You obviously haven't heard about them.'

'Is someone trying to fix me?'

'I'm afraid it seems like it,' Gregg said inventively.

'Whoever's talking is a bleeding liar.'

'He saw you out late that night and you were cold sober.'

'I wasn't,' he shouted, 'I was boozed.'

Edna threw open the door. 'What's he saying now, Perce?'

'Someone's telling him I wasn't on the booze.'

She faced Gregg. 'Mister, it don't matter what's said. When Perce came back here, he was too far gone to get up the stairs to bed.'

'When did he arrive?'

'It wasn't short of midnight; woke me up. It don't matter what anyone says, Perce was so stifled he couldn't have nicked from a blind man.'

She had spoken without her earlier belligerence, rather with the intensity of someone desperate to make the listener understand she was telling the truth.

'Perce,' Greg said, 'maybe you didn't do the Querry job, but were busy somewhere else? If that wasn't a big deal, admit it because the court can consider the small size of the theft and that it's not done much harm to anyone.'

'He was on the booze,' Edna said again, now with dull despair.

'Their story hasn't changed, Sarge,' Gregg said as he stood in front of Warren's desk.

Warren fiddled with a pencil.

'I reckon they're telling the truth. Perce was drinking heavily for much of the evening and he arrived home incapable near midnight.'

'The job was done so sharply it had to be a top peterman; Perce and Gutteridge are the only local ones.'

'Why does he have to be a local?'

'We've argued that one out.'

'And could be wrong. The Irwins maybe don't publicize their house, but he's a big noise in the City . . .'

'How d'you know that?'

'She said he was working in the City when I called to make the security survey. You've got to be big before you live in a place like Querry Brade and your wife has enough jewellery to cover herself from head to toe. Maybe some smart peterman organized the job on speculation; the house hasn't had any publicity, but there's every chance she's been photographed at one of those big parties City tycoons go to with their wives and someone saw her and said to himself, That's worth a look-see. The daily may be a hundred per cent, but she may have a loose tongue. Any one of the gardeners on contract work who's been there must have some idea of what's inside and has talked after a few beers.'

'And I can provide another dozen possibilities which will be just as useless. County HQ has been on to the guv'nor wanting to know what progress there's been and since he had to tell them that for the moment we're stalled, they're unhappy and he's breathing fire. Why haven't we identified the second man? Wouldn't listen to the problems of doing so. All Mr Irwin could say was that he was a big man who took orders. That – as I've said before, but no one was listening – makes him pure muscle, no brain. So we have to run through records and identify all possible suspects and start questioning them, which takes for ever. No excuse, the guv'nor says. If it isn't, what the bloody hell is?'

As he left, Gregg reflected that ill humour, like leaking guttering water, dribbled down.

Warren entered the DI's room.

'What is it?' Horton said sharply.

'We've received a request for a security survey from a small supermarket in Nessden-on-Sea. I'd like your advice, sir.'

'You're incapable of making decisions?'

'I thought that because of what's happened—'

'Was a series of incidents which it was our duty to investigate, despite my judgment that when viewed together, they did not incriminate a member of our team.'

Rank, Gregg thought, easily shed responsibility for mistakes. 'Then I go ahead as usual?'

'Is there reason for not doing so?'

'I have your authority to send Gregg to make the survey on the store?'

'You do not need my authority for that. What is the

problem? You still have doubts, despite the lack of evidence of Gregg's guilt?'

'From the beginning, I said—'

'Or do you want to cover yourself? Do you know what happens to a man who tries to ride two horses at the same time?'

'I am no horseman,' Warren said resentfully.

'He falls flat on his arse.'

The church clock, heard when the wind was in the right direction, struck midday as Lodge reached the pawn shop. He entered. Not long before, the shop had been on the point of closing through lack of business, but the end of free-and-easy credit had resulted in an increase of trade.

The broad, strapping woman with bright red hair was infamous for the day two layabouts had thought to rob the till. She had broken the nose of one before both ran, empty-handed. 'Not seen you for a while, Mr Lodge,' she said, her voice deep and gravelly.

'You've scared every villain away so there's no excuse for us coming to see you.'

She laughed, a deep, belly laugh which had her un-secured breasts straining at the bright blue blouse she wore. 'So how's life been for you?'

'I could complain, but who would listen? . . . We're asking around if any of the jewellery from the Querry Brade job is reaching the market.'

'Not here, it isn't. And who's going to walk in and try to pawn a Russian tiara?'

'Could be someone stupid enough not to know what it is.' He handed her a copy of the list of stolen jewellery. 'Perhaps you'll keep this handy and give us a bell if anything on it appears?'

She skimmed through the descriptions. 'All right, dear, but it's way out of my class. The stuff I'm shown is always called priceless and I have to tell 'em, that's true because it's not worth anything.' Another deep belly laugh.

He thanked her, left. A couple of hundred yards down

the road was a fish-and-chip shop. According to Guinevere, the kind of place where only 'they' went. She would not serve chips at home because they were so fattening; in a restaurant, she insisted he did not order them because then she would be unable to resist eating some. She loved to tempt, but not to be tempted.

He walked on, passed a woman he knew to be a prostitute. There were times – usually after Guinevere had encouraged, but vindictively refused – when frustration had edged him towards finding professional relief. Yet he had never done so because, absurdly, he feared she might learn it and leave him.

If only: the most useless of words. If only he could release himself from his need for her.

He stopped in front of a travel agent. Behind the window were cards on which were details of holidays. Eight nights in Barcelona; six in Paris; a weekend in Naples; a round trip to New York, plane outward, liner home. He went inside. On the left was the counter behind which two women worked; on his right, four racks filled with brochures. A package holiday of ten days in Jamaica cost £645. It would be £1,290 for the two of them. And that was without adding on the amount of money she would spend there. Yet she demanded not a package holiday, but one accompanying Cynthia and Phillip. That must cost twice, thrice as much. She had to understand it was impossible.

He returned to the CID general room as Gregg was about to leave. 'What's moving?' he asked.

'Me. Several men to question and find out if they were the heavyweight on the Querry job and a security survey in Nessden.'

'There used to be a delicatessen there where Guinevere liked to shop because much of the food was imported from France. But it closed down some years ago. She says that was because the town has become downmarket, catering for the ancients.'

'It's the pensioners who still have money to spend.'

'Unlike us soldiers, holding the line between civilization and anarchy.'

'What on earth has you talking that kind of cod's?

'My innate literary genius.'

Fourteen

Simpson had the build of a blacksmith. His broken nose was evidence of the time he had been employed as a bouncer, the scar on his left cheek of a knife fight he had almost lost. 'Why you asking?' he sullenly demanded as he leaned against a fork-lift at the back of a block of flats under construction.

'To hear you answer,' Gregg replied, having to speak loudly to overcome the increased noise of machinery.

'You ain't got nothing on me.'

'Four convictions and one not guilty when the jury consisted of eleven idiots and one deaf and dumb.'

'Can't leave a bloke alone.'

'A complaint I hear every day of the year.'

'I'm going straight.'

'Like a car on full lock?'

'Can't you bleeding well see I'm working here?'

'Since when?'

'Three months.'

A man hurried towards them, shouting, 'You ain't paid to stand around.' He came to a stop. 'And you. What the hell you think you're doing here?'

'Having a word with Mr Simpson,' Gregg replied.

'This ain't a public meeting place. Clear off before I have you thrown off.'

'Inadvisable.'

'Smart, are you?'

'CID.'

The foreman hesitated. 'You've a warrant card?' he finally asked.

Gregg showed it to him.

'There's some sort of trouble?' He stared at Simpson.

It was the policy never to leave room for suspicion when there was no good reason to do so. 'Mr Simpson may have witnessed an accident and we need to know if he can help us decide what caused it.'

The foreman spoke uneasily. 'Sorry about me threatening. Wouldn't have happened if you'd said who you was at the beginning.'

'No harm done since you didn't try to put words into action.'

He walked away.

'I ain't seen no accident,' Simpson said.

'No, but it's better he left thinking you had, rather than that I was questioning you officially since that might have persuaded him to get rid of you.'

Simpson considered what had been said. 'Questioning me about what?'

'Where you were last Saturday night, Sunday morning.'

'Working.'

'Throughout the night?'

'Course not.'

'Let's become more specific. Saturday night.'

'What about it?'

'Don't be too dense or I'll have you along for a mental check to see if you're safe enough to mix with the public.'

'You mean, where was I?'

'Congratulations.'

'I was here, working.'

'Until when?'

'Five. They don't want Saturday evening or Sunday work because of the cost of overtime.'

'What did you do when you finished work?'

'What you trying to pin on me?'

'You worked as a heavy before you spent time as a bouncer.'

'Don't touch it now.'

'Not when it's easy money? Like tying up an old couple who can't offer any opposition?'

'I keep telling you, I ain't done a job since I started work.'

'That sounds illogical.'

'What are you on about now?'

'Let's go back to Saturday night. Where did you go when you finished here?'

'Home.'

'And later on?'

'What you trying to line me up for?'

'Querry Brade. Tell me you've never heard of the place and I'll take you in straight away as the heavy.'

'You think I was in on that?'

'You catch on quickly.'

Simpson spoke at length with bitter anger. A bloke made one mistake and the coppers were on to him like a fox on to a chicken. They wouldn't leave him alone, not if he wore a halo. All they wanted was to send someone down and it didn't matter if he was innocent, just so long as he couldn't prove that. Well, he sodding well could prove he hadn't been on that job – or any other – whatever any bastard said.

'Try me.'

'I was in France.'

'Dating Joan of Arc?'

'Three of us took a van across and stocked up with beer and whisky. Ask 'em in the shop where we bought the stuff, they'll remember. Ask the custom sods who tried to say we was bringing the stuff back to sell.'

'When did you return?'

'Next morning.'

'You were buying all night long?'

'Went on to a kind of club.'

'What kind?'

'Strippers. Me mates wanted to go there.'

'You didn't?'

'Don't like that kind of thing. Don't seem right the girls should show themselves to a load of boozy men.'

That was such an unexpected sentiment that Gregg knew it had to be true. Further enquiries would have to be made,

but he accepted that Simpson had not been the heavy in
the robbery.

Nessden-on-Sea had been a prosperous town between the
Edwardian era and the outbreak of World War Two. Later, as
with so many seaside resorts, people who had become more
prosperous flew to the Mediterranean where sun, sea, sand –
and for many of the younger, sex – were all but guaranteed.

Hotels slowly deteriorated, shops lost custom and lowered
the quality of the goods they stocked.

The turnaround had begun when the need for change was
finally accepted and hotels adapted to the needs of the grey
generation. TV sets in every bedroom and public room
providing an endless and mindless way of passing time; bingo
halls which did this with the added allure of profit. Life, or
more accurately the approach of death, had fuelled the revival.

Gregg parked at the rear of Murray's Superstore. Warren
had termed it a small supermarket, but appearance suggested
this was only true in comparison with some. The offices
were at the back of the typically ugly, windowless building.
A smart young lady, making it clear she was not a potential pick-up, asked him to wait while she spoke to the
manager. Moments later, Gregg was in an office in which
were a safe, half a dozen VDUs showing different parts of
the store, and the usual equipment. He asked the manager
questions relating to security and gained the impression he
had been called more so the other could demonstrate his
initiative than because there was much fear of theft.

The survey took time. At the conclusion, Gregg made his
recommendations. The selling space was well covered, the
office and storeroom not so. He advised these last two be
better protected. More importantly, the lead-in of the electrical cable which fed the security equipment needed better
protection. The free-standing safe was modern and proof
against any peterman of normal ability. The Sunday takings
were left in this overnight; on all other nights, the money
was collected, after the store closed to the public, by
armoured van belonging to a private firm. He said it would

be better if this was also the routine on Sunday nights, was told the firm would not work then.

He left Nessden to drive to divisional HQ, feeling like he'd just wasted his time.

When the art of cooking was reduced to putting prepared food into the microwave and setting the timer correctly, Guinevere was an adequate cook. Lodge finished the last of the roast beef and Yorkshire pudding, looked across the dining-room table – she refused to eat in the kitchen – and asked, 'What's for afters?'

'Dessert.'

'Sorry.'

'Why can't you leave your working manners back at work?'

Diners at the canteen at HQ did not eat with their fingers and throw the bones over their shoulders, à la Henry VIII, but she preferred to believe that they did. In any case, he was not going to correct her since he needed her in a pleasant mood.

'There are gooseberry tarts on the kitchen table. They need warming and you can open a tin of custard.'

He went through to the kitchen. The tarts were still in their wrappers, on which was the price, on the table, as were those from the roast beef and Yorkshire pudding. Proof of why they were always trying to keep up with their expenses.

He returned to the dining room, handed her one plate, put the second in front of his seat, the tin of custard in the centre of the table.

'A tin on the table? For God's sake, show some manners and empty it into a jug.'

'I thought to save washing up.'

'You didn't think because you don't know.'

He picked up the tin, went through to the kitchen and did as ordered. He should have kept his mind on the present, not on the past and possible future.

'Jenny rang this afternoon,' she said, as he sat.

'Oh?'

'You aren't interested?'

'Of course I am. How is she?'

'The same as ever.'

Another Cynthia. Empty-headed, lived by her horoscope, married to a rich man.

'She and Howard are off to Malaya because he's some work there.'

'They go abroad a lot.'

'We're the only ones who don't.'

The conversation had not gone as he had hoped.

Warren spoke to the detective inspector. 'Two more reports on petermen have come through from other forces, sir.'

'Why only two?'

'I suppose, as always, people are taking their time. After all, a robbery down here doesn't directly concern another force.'

'No excuse for slackness.'

Which was rich. Horton would never give priority to providing information other forces had requested.

'Are you going to give me the reports or continue standing there dumb?'

Warren wondered if Horton's wife was suffering as much bad humour as was CID. 'Two names provided, one's in jail, the other retired after getting his active hand mashed in machinery.'

'The chief super is wondering if we're all asleep down here.'

'I don't see what else we can do.'

'Nail the bastards.'

There was a long silence. 'And no one's near naming the heavy?' Horton's mood had changed to sour pessimism.

'The lads are out, asking around. But it's bound to take time.'

'Something has to break our way.'

A man had to be truly pessimistic to believe that.

Fifteen

It was the middle of September and the weather remained warm and dry; had done so for long enough for water restrictions to have been imposed. Guinevere stood by the opened window of the bedroom. 'Isn't that wonderful!'

Lodge, having no idea what she was talking about, sat on the edge of the bed and hoped her present mood would continue.

'The nightingale's song is ethereal.'

'A nightingale at this time of year?' *She all night long her amorous descant sung.*

'Does everything female have to be sexy? . . . I could listen for hours and hours.'

'And miss your beauty sleep?'

'I suppose you think I need that?'

'There's no one needs it less.'

'You're suddenly very gallant.'

'Can't be anything else with you in the bedroom.' His optimism increased because she had spoken lightly.

'I suppose I'd better get to bed because it may sing for hours. I do hope it returns tomorrow night. But I don't suppose it will since it's a miracle to hear one in the centre of a town.' She drew the curtains across the window, walked to the far side of the bed and undressed provocatively. She hung up her clothes. 'Do you think I'm putting on weight?'

'Not half an ounce.'

'Mandy thinks I have.'

'Only because she knows she is obviously getting fatter and is jealously trying to gain the pleasure of upsetting you.'

'She is stretching her clothes a little. Or maybe that's being kind and it's more than a little. She cannot stop eating chocolate.' She walked slowly around the bed, reached under the pillows and brought out a nightdress. 'I bought this this morning so you haven't seen it.' She pulled it over her head, giggled as it became caught when only halfway down.

The panels of lacework had been designed by a sadist, he decided. A man who understood that what was half seen was more intriguing than that which was fully exposed.

She climbed into bed, did not pick up a paperback. 'Cynthia phoned this afternoon. She said it was just for a chat, but what she really wanted was cattishly to remind me they'd quite soon be off to Jamaica and that they'll be there for four weeks.'

'I thought it was only going to be for two?'

'Something's happened at work which means Phillip can have the extra time. Cynthia had to mention that gave us a better chance of seeing them there. She knows we can't afford it, the bitch.'

'Maybe she was wasting her bile.'

'How?'

'I was passing Caxton's this afternoon – the travel agent in Edley Street – and in the window was the notice of a forthcoming cruise. Fares are so reasonable because it's what they call a promotional cruise. It's the ship's maiden voyage so they want to make certain everything is working.'

'My parents were on the maiden voyage of the *Queen Mary*.'

When they must have been children and probably had not even met. She never understood how absurd many of her claims so obviously were. 'Do you remember on the telly that programme about a luxury liner being built? I think she's that ship.'

She thought for a moment. 'The one with a fabulous shopping centre and all the top names in it?'

'That's the picture. Instead of going to Torremolinos—'

'I never wanted to go there and meet the most ghastly people.'

'The cruise would make up for not being able to join
Cynthia and Phillip.'

'If we can afford a cruise, why can't we join them for
part of their stay?'

'It's not like that. And when you think about it, thousands go to Jamaica, but only a very few people sail on a
maiden voyage. That would really be something to talk
about!'

'It would certainly upset Cynthia. She can't ever have
done that or she'd talk about it all the time . . . I've always
wanted to see Japan. They make such wonderful things in
silk which are so reasonable. Or is that China? . . . No, it's
Hong Kong. Mary bought that frock there which she wears
so she can boast about its being silk. Is it going to the Far
East?'

'A ship is always feminine.'

'Why?'

'Because she goes faster with four screws than one.'

'You can be so crude.'

She had spoken without malice. He said, 'I'm afraid she's
not going to the Far East.'

'Where, then? New York?'

'Madeira.'

'And after that?'

'Back to Southampton.'

'You're saying it's only going that far?' Her voice rose
and her tone became shrill. 'You call that a cruise?'

'It's a promotional trip which is why it's not too long
and doesn't cost a fortune. Maybe we won't visit anywhere
but Madeira, but I've read it's a wonderful island. And we'll
have three days at sea there and back . . .'

'Who the hell wants to stare at the sea for day after day?'

'There are deck games, swimming pools, a theatre, a
cinema, three restaurants – one of which has twenty-four-
hour service—'

'And you expect me to sit at a table with you God knows
how many times a day while you pig into the food while
I have to go without?'

'You'll enjoy all those shops.'

'When you'll keep telling me we can't afford what I want?'

'But—'

'I tell people I've been on a cruise, they say how wonderful, where did you go, what did you see, and I have to tell them just Madeira. How bloody humiliating would that be? But you never think about my feelings. I'd rather go for a trip on the ferry to the Isle of Wight.'

'I didn't think—'

'Of course you didn't. You saw a cruise that wasn't a cruise and so dirt cheap even *you* could afford it and that was all that mattered.'

The torture of lingering, aching passion. This time, he would not give in to it. He would find the will power to forget the sight of her undressing, walking naked about the room, deliberately exciting him . . . Did a heroin addict give up his drug merely by telling himself he would?

Sixteen

The Transit van had been in the council car park by the side of Murray's Superstore since five on Saturday evening. Despite notices forbidding parking through the night, drivers of commercial vehicles found it convenient to park there over the weekend, and the Transit went unremarked.

At one in the morning, the rear doors opened and three men climbed out on to the tarmac, their movements obscured by the building, a tall privet hedge, and four other vehicles left there for the night. They moved arms and legs to ease the effects of a cramped vigil, drew in deep breaths of salty air to clear away the fug of body odours which they had had to endure.

They crossed to the door that provided direct access to the offices. The geography of the site was greatly in their favour as they could work in the shadow cast by the building. One man held a hand spray, intended for plants, and pumped up the internal pressure; he aimed the muzzle at the brickwork just above the tarmac, three measured feet from the door. The surface of the brick fizzed as the acid ate into it. When that activity subsided, a second man used a wooden spatula to brush aside the eroded brickwork to leave a fresh surface, and in turn, this was sprayed. A hammer and chisel would have done the job more quickly, but even with padded tools, there would have been noise.

Two electric cables were revealed. About to cut the one easier to reach, a sharp word of warning reminded the man he had to cut the second one. The lights in the store remained on, but the alarms in the office complex were now out of action.

Several keys were tried on the lock of the door, but it was of a complex, strong construction. Small holes were hand-drilled around where the inner lock was judged to lie; a keyhole saw cut out the circle; a skilful twist brought out the lock with engaged tongue.

The complex consisted of two small offices and a bathroom. The free-standing safe was in the first office. Four feet tall, three feet wide and deep, it had the appearance of impregnability.

Curtains, of a very uninspired pattern, were drawn across the single window. The men had brought a large blanket with them and this was hung over the curtains. The thieves' maxim – if you're certain something is safe, it isn't.

The peterman was of moderate height, moderate build, and moderate appearance. In a group of two, he would go unremarked. That was, unless one chanced to notice his fingers. These were unusually long and thin, the nails were manicured, the skin was almost as smooth as the proverbial baby's bottom. He stood by the safe, waiting, as the other two searched the drawers in the desk, the sides and back of the desk, the company files in the small bookcase, looking for a hidden note of the safe's combination. When the search failed, the peterman stripped off his gloves, put them down on his small hold-all, drew from that what appeared to be a large fountain pen, a small electric drill, and a laptop computer which he placed on a chair that had been moved close to the safe.

As the other two watched, from time to time nervously ducking under the blanket and curtains to make certain all remained quiet outside, he drilled a fine hole above the combination dial, opened the 'fountain pen' to expose a very thin steel rod which he inserted into the hole. He switched on the laptop and opened a file – it had taken him years to perfect this – which would provide, when he fed in numbers gained from turning the combination wheel and probing the lock with the steel rod, the mathematically deduced combination number. With all his experience, it still took him just over three hours to open the safe. The dial was rubbed with an anti-grease solvent to erase any prints, or parts of prints, which had been left, even though the ribbed surface made this very unlikely.

The bank notes had been bundled into different denominations. A rough estimate suggested they had gained more than expected. The store had clearly enjoyed extensive trade that Sunday morning.

They checked and re-checked they were leaving no object, no mark which could be incriminating. They left through the outside doorway and were walking towards the van when a patrolling constable, who had turned in to the car park from a small path between bingo hall and furniture store, saw them. He activated the radio attached to his jacket, reported as he ran forward, careless that he faced three men, one of whom was noticeably larger than he. It would have been far more prudent, having given the alarm, to challenge them from a distance, but there was no room for prudence when a crime was being committed.

He made the mistake of assuming the short, slightly-built man offered the least danger and ignored him as he closed with the other two. A knife sliced into his side and as he fell, the pain became furnace-hot.

'You bloody fool!'

'*Rien que la merde,*' said the peterman as he kicked the dying constable.

Seventeen

Warren stepped into the DI's office. 'PC Mullins has just reported through that Quale died fifteen minutes ago.'

Horton looked through the window. A rising pigeon flew past. Like Quale's soul ascending? He didn't believe in inner selves surviving death, he didn't believe in heaven or hell, but the image remained.

'Would you like me to speak to the widow, sir?'

'That's my job. And how the hell do I carry it out? I never know what to say, not even after so many years. How can words begin to touch her pain? What can our commiserations mean to her?'

'Words are said to help.'

'If your wife had just been murdered and someone came along to say how sorry he was, would you feel one iota less grief?'

'I doubt it.'

Time passed before Horton said, 'What you can do is later on, when the time seems right, help the widow put in her claim for compensation.'

'Of course.'

'And because we live in a world where justice lies in the eyes of the bureaucratic beholder, she'll get less than some red-eyed female will be awarded for unjust dismissal . . . Did Quale say anything before he died?'

'He regained a measure of consciousness and struggled to speak. Mullins did his best to understand, but all he could make out was the one word, "fog". Quale died a moment later.'

'Fog. What does that say to you?'

'Can't make it out, sir, unless he was saying he couldn't remember anything because of the fog in his mind.'

'Would a dying man struggle to tell someone that?'

'I was by the bedside of a man who said "Strawberries" immediately before he died.'

'And you never understood why he said that?'

'No.'

'To get back to the world we live in. Two facts stick out. The peterman was not just good, he was in a class of his own since these days his ilk are mostly too lazy to earn the hard way; robbing a bank at gunpoint is so much simpler. Out of all the names we've collected, how many are capable of tackling a very good, modern combination safe?'

'Could be two. But one's in jail and the other is presumed dead. I've had a word with the force concerned. They have no doubt he is dead, but there's no hard proof of that.'

'Then in effect, you are saying we have no named suspect. Yet someone as talented as this man can't be anonymous. Have every snout questioned again. Ask all forces to pull their combined fingers out and go through the files more carefully.'

'I'll do that, sir, but—'

'But me no buts.' Horton shifted in his chair, seeking a more comfortable position. 'It's obvious the villains knew exactly where to break through the wall in order to cut the electricity to the office. Get me the report on the security which Gregg drew up.'

Warren left and Horton stared into space. He had condemned himself for believing in Gregg's guilt; then the evidence had restored – or appeared to restore – the other's innocence. Had Quale died because he had been too ready to accept this and allow Gregg to make the survey?

Warren returned and passed across the report.

'Have you re-read it?' Horton asked.

'Yes, sir.'

'And?'

Warren spoke reluctantly. 'The potential vulnerability of the incoming cable to the alarm system is detailed.'

'Your conclusion?'

'The villains did not break through the wall at the right place by chance.'

Detective Chief Superintendent McGill was a large man whose bulk was evenly distributed so that he did not appear to be fat. His facial features were sharp, though not as sharp as his tongue could be; his eyes were the cold blue of arctic waters; his nose was aquiline; his mouth suggested he found smiling difficult. Yet if his reputation at work was that of a hard bastard who was interested only in success, his family knew him as warm-hearted, generous, and amusing.

He did not flaunt his rank. He knocked on the door and waited to be asked in. Horton hurriedly came to his feet. 'Good morning, sir. You've made very good time.'

'Not much traffic.'

'I'll move a chair . . .'

'No need.' McGill picked up one of the chairs against the wall, set this in front of the desk, sat.

'PC Mullins reported in an hour and a half, or so, ago. Very sadly, PC Quale died in hospital.'

'I heard on the radio. Has the widow been informed?'

'I'm just back from telling her.'

'The worst job a policeman has to do.'

There was a brief silence as each remembered a moment, or moments, when their luck might have run out and their wives would be given the news which ruined their lives.

Horton broke the reverie. 'Before he died, Quale tried to speak to Mullins, but unfortunately he was virtually incomprehensible. All Mullins could understand was the one word "fog".'

'Does that mean anything to you?'

'There's no operation under progress with that code name. Quale would surely have been trying to identify, or give information which would identify, his killer, but we've no name on the books that's even close to Fog.

'As to the rest, daylight searching in and around the outside of the supermarket, questioning of nearby residents to learn if they saw or heard anything, notices around the car park asking the public to help, questioning local villains who might have taken part – all have been carried out or are in progress.'

'With any success?'

'Not so far.'

'Then you have no lead?'

'Unfortunately, there is one, sir.'

'That's a bloody strange way of putting things.'

'I think it will become clear when I say that back at the beginning of June, DC Gregg carried out a security survey of Querry Brade, owned by wealthy people, in which was a very valuable collection of jewellery—'

'You think I'm unaware of all that? Or of the fact you seem to have made no progress in weeks?'

'We've had little to go on, sir . . . There was existing security, but Gregg judged it would hardly keep a tearaway kid out and he detailed a modern, highly efficient system which needed to be installed immediately.

'The house was robbed five days later, before any work on updating security had been carried out. It seemed a strange coincidence that the robbery should have taken place in the short window of time when it could easily be carried out, but we accepted that this sort of thing happens. Then the rumour was picked up that the job had been carried out using information provided by a policeman.'

McGill's anger was sharp. 'Why was I not informed immediately?'

'At that point, sir, the probability had to be the rumour was false, maliciously introduced to blacken our name. However, I carried out an investigation, with the help of Sergeant Warren. We started off with the premise that if the rumour was true, the obvious suspect was Gregg, since he had drawn up a detailed description of the existing security, listing all its faults. In the process of doing that, he naturally provided a useful description of the house. We compared all the security surveys Gregg had made to see if there were later thefts from the same houses. There was no match.'

'You accepted that as proof of innocence, ignoring the fact Querry Brade might be the first time he sold information?'

'We considered it not proof, but a negative that was almost as good. We knew him as a first-class officer without a question mark in his records.'

'Yet you started by questioning him.'

'Only because the rumour had to be followed up and if there had been a sale of information, he had to be the prime suspect.'

McGill lit a cigarette, careless of rules against smoking in public places. 'Since the good name of the police was concerned, you should have informed me immediately.'

'I thought—'

'That to do so would put you in the unwelcome limelight, so first find out what really happened. What I want to know now is, why have you finally seen fit to tell me about all this?'

'Gregg carried out a security survey on Murray's Superstore.'

'You have a copy of his report?'

Horton stood, carried the report round to McGill, returned to his seat. Having read the pages, McGill dropped them on his lap. 'The villains cut into the brickwork at the exact point where they needed to. And can you suggest how they would have known there was a separate electrical supply to the office without access to this report?'

'No, sir.'

'We'll question him at eight this evening.'

Gregg phoned Wendy on the mobile. 'How are things?'

'Bumpy. Junior is practising for the high jump.'

'Be grateful it's not the pole vault.'

'It's such a pity men can't have babies.'

'Divine mercy. I'm ringing to say I'll be back late tonight.'

'Something's happening?'

'The copper who was knifed early this morning has died.'

'God, how awful. Did you know him?'

'Only by sight and the odd pleasantry.'

'Was he married?'

'Yes, with a young kid.'

'Will someone be trying to help them?'

'They will.'

'Are you going to have to be down in Nessden?'

'I'm to hang on here for the moment because the chief superintendent wants a word with me. Which is like hearing one's death sentence read out.'

'For heaven's sake, why say that?'

'He breathes napalm and incinerates constables who annoy him.'

'Then arm yourself with a lance . . . How have you annoyed him?'

'As far as I know, I haven't.'

'Then maybe he's going to tell you you've been promoted.'

'Maybe the earth really is flat.'

Gregg waited in the CID room. Chappell, fingering his beard, said, 'The sarge has been on at me again.'

'To do some work?'

'To get rid of my beard. Says it makes me look like a pirate.'

'He has a point.'

'I've been wondering if that's why I've got to see the super tomorrow. Maybe he's going to revoke my permission to wear a beard.'

'At a time like this, he won't bother if you wear a cutlass between your teeth. In any case, I've gathered he's seeing all of us.'

'Why's he want to do that?'

'I expect it's to give us a pep talk and tell us to work harder.'

'He thinks he has to do that when we're doing everything in our powers to catch the bastard who murdered Ted Quale?'

'The brass like to believe they can stir emotions with heroic words.'

'You don't think it's more likely to have something to do with the rumour going around that information from here is being sold?'

'Even if he is from county HQ, he can't be stupid enough to believe that's possible.' Gregg looked at his watch. 'He's ten minutes late already.'

'Complain when you see him.'

'And start the napalm flowing?'

'I heard he once—' Chappell stopped short as Warren entered the room.

'Gregg, Interview One.' Warren went out, slammed the door shut behind him.

'So warm and friendly!' Chappell said.

'Perhaps his kid is in trouble again.'

Gregg left and made his way downstairs. Above each of the interview rooms was an illuminated indicator – both showed the rooms were unoccupied. Gregg entered No. 1. He sat on the interviewee's chair – for the first time – and with nothing to occupy him, appreciated how oppressive the room was, how readily it might exacerbate a feeling of guilt. Walls in two tones of brown; the one small window barred; the framed list of interviewees' rights, badly stained; the wooden chairs and scarred table of institutional design and quality.

McGill and Horton entered, Gregg stood. Horton switched on the recording machine, increasing Gregg's uneasiness – this was to be no casual interview.

McGill spoke in a quiet, even voice. 'We're asking you, and others, to answer questions of very considerable importance. You will answer them as fully as you can. Is that clear?'

'Yes, sir.'

'You know there has been a rumour that the robbery at Querry Brade was so successful because information had been supplied to the villains by someone in this force?'

'Yes, sir.'

'How did you judge the rumour when you heard it?'

'As some joker trying to blacken our name.'

'You did not consider it might contain at least some truth?'

'That was impossible.'

'One always wants to believe that, but, sadly, experience shows there can be a rotten apple.'

'Not in this manor, sir.'

'Why so confident?'

'I'm speaking for CID. There isn't one of us could ever become a traitor, whatever the circumstances. We're a tight, friendly team and if one of us was on the black, the rest of us would very soon become suspicious.'

'And if suspicious?'

'He would report his suspicions.'

'However unproven they were?'

'Obviously, I can only say for sure what I would do. But I'll bet any of the others would do exactly the same.'

'Will you accept there is reason to fear there may be some truth in the rumour?'

After a while, Gregg said, 'If I have to.'

'Then clearly we have to consider how the information which was sold could have been gathered. The best way of doing that is to consider the specific case of Querry Brade. You were asked by the owner to conduct a security survey of the house and grounds. You did so, in considerable detail, and in conclusion suggested what needed to be done to improve security. Did you make notes while going around the house?'

'Yes, sir.'

'What happened to them?'

'I returned here and drew up my report with their help.'

'Did you file them?'

'I put them through the shedder since I no longer needed them.'

'Your report was drawn up on a computer?'

'On my computer.'

'Are you saying no one else uses it?'

'Since my work could be very confidential, it was agreed no one else in the room was to use it.'

'Is your work encoded?'

'When necessary.'

'Which is when?'

'When it deals with things such as security surveys.'

'You employ a secure system of encoding?'

'Yes, sir.'

'Who knows the key to unlocking the encoded information?'

'I do.'

'Naturally. I am asking, who else?'

'No one.'

'Should you suffer a fatal accident, your work could not be retrieved?'

'I spoke to Sergeant Warren when I was first made security officer. I suggested I wrote out the key, sealed it in an envelope to be kept in the station's safe. He agreed.'

'How many copies of a security survey do you print out?'

'To begin with, one. That is taken to Sergeant Warren so he can order any alterations he considers necessary.'

'He hands you back this copy and you enter any alterations on your computer. What do you then do with that copy?'

'Shred it.'

'How many corrected copies do you print?'

'Two. One for Sergeant Warren, one for the owner of the property.'

'Not one for yourself?'

'There is no need for that. The information is on the hard disk.'

'Could someone else read what you were writing as you worked at the computer?'

'No one would try. But no, no one could.'

'Why so certain?'

'I sit with my back to the wall.'

'What if you have reason to leave the room when in the middle of drawing up a report?'

'I encode what has been written before I leave.'

'The screen is never clear for anyone else?'

'Never.'

McGill turned to Horton. 'Have you any questions?'

'No, sir.'

'Who's next?'

'Constable Chappell.'

He looked at his watch. 'We'll speak to him tomorrow morning.'

'Right, sir.'

He turned back to Gregg. 'Thank you for your help.'

Gregg made his way up to the general room. Chappell, who regarded paperwork as the curse of the devil, was making out a 21a form, explaining why form 21 had been incompletely made out. He said, 'Well?'

'You were right. It is about the rumour.'

'What did you tell him?'

'That it was ridiculous. Before I forget, you're going to be called into the lion's den tomorrow morning.'

'Why waste time with all this nonsense? Are they so thick they can't see we're not crook? That it's a hundred times more important to catch the bastard who murdered Quale?'

'They must reckon there's some connection.'

'Such as what?'

'I've no more idea than you have.'

'How did you find the chief super?'

'Quite pleasant for a top brass.'

'Trying to fool me?'

'There wasn't so much as a growl from him.'

'Must be your baby face.'

'Virtue has its own rewards.'

'Boredom.'

Minutes later, Gregg phoned Wendy. 'I'm on my way.'

'You had me thinking your dragon had incinerated you.'

'McGill doesn't live up to his reputation.'

Eighteen

Monday was a grey, gloomy day, reminding people that 'Life is real! Life is earnest.' Interview room No. 1 might have been waiting for the undertaker to call.

'You understand?' McGill asked.

'Yes, sir,' Lodge replied.

'So what is your response?'

'It has to be nonsense. No one in our team would sell as much as yesterday's paper to a villain.'

'I didn't restrict the possibility to CID.'

'I can't say I know everyone in uniform well, but that's of no account. It will be the same for them.'

'So you dismiss out of hand the possibility there could be any truth in the rumour?'

'Yes, sir.'

'Then can you suggest how it might have arisen?'

'Some smart villain just out of the slammer thinking it would be fun to put the black on us.'

McGill picked up a pencil and began to tap it against the palm of his other hand. 'Do you have anything to do with security surveys? Do you sometimes help DC Gregg with the actual survey or the drawing up of the recommendations if it's a particularly large or difficult job?'

'If it was Buck House, he wouldn't accept any help. He couldn't be more security conscious. Sometimes wonder if he allows himself to trust himself.'

'Presumably he discusses his work in-house?'

'He might say where he's going or just been, but that's an end of it. Never a mention of anything important.'

'You had no idea what a rich haul the jewellery in Querry Brade offered?'

'Until the robbery, I'm fairly certain I hadn't ever heard the name of the house.'

'Then DC Gregg did not mention he was about to conduct, or had, a survey there?'

'His only mention was to say he was off to do a security survey.'

'If you were asked to describe the relationship between the three of you in CID, how would you do so?'

'I'd say we're a good team, ready to give a hand to each other, any time, anywhere.'

'No question marks?'

'How do you mean, sir?'

'There's never been any reason for you to wonder about the others' work or private lives?'

Lodge did not immediately answer.

'Well?'

'Sir, if you're asking me whether I suspect any of them could have sold information, the answer is no, I'd as soon suspect myself.'

McGill's questions became less direct.

It was just after midday when Chappell strode into the interview room, red beard thrust forward as if preparing for battle.

'Sit down,' McGill said.

He sat.

'You will no doubt have heard why I am questioning all of you?'

'Yes. And if you think—' He stopped.

'If I think what?'

'Nothing, sir.'

'A somewhat explosive reaction to nothing. I understand you were told by a snout that the theft at Querry Brade relied on information sold by a copper?'

'Yes.'

'How did you respond to what he said?'

'Told him if he ever said anything like that to anyone else, I'd push his head up . . . Said he was a liar and to keep his mouth shut.'

'Did you think there might be a grain of truth in the story?'

'Of course not.'

'It can happen that a policeman turns crook.'

'Not here it can't.'

'Why not?'

'Because we're a team.'

'I've been told the same thing by others.'

'Then maybe you'll start believing it.'

'Watch your tongue,' Warren snapped.

'Let him talk,' McGill said. 'Did you know DC Gregg was carrying out a security survey at Querry Brade?'

The following questions were similar to those which Gregg had been asked; so were the answers.

Chappell left.

McGill stood, began to pace the floor clear of the table. 'I've never trusted beards. Don't know why.'

'You can trust him, sir,' Warren said. 'Reliable, a solid worker, can be a little hot-headed, though.'

'Hardly an ideal trait in a police officer.'

Or of beards? Warren wondered.

'What have we gained from the questioning?'

'Other than that no one harbours any suspicions, not very much.'

'Bloody nothing! Yet until we can be certain information was sold and not rely on rumours and a broad distrust of coincidences, we're not going to get anywhere.' He came to a stop. 'Anything from Nessden?'

'Nothing fresh, sir.'

'We'll go through all the information we have again in case we've missed something or to confirm there's nothing to be missed. Was it the same mob who did the supermarket and murdered Quale as did the Querry job? We can't judge.'

Warren spoke diffidently. 'I don't think it was because . . . I've had an idea, sir.'

McGill was slightly surprised, having summed up Warren as a man without much imagination.

'I'm afraid it's rather far-fetched . . .'

'It can have come from the Solomon Islands if it offers a chance of identifying the killer.'

'Returning from Nessden, I was briefly close to the Eurostar track and a train passed at a thousand miles an hour. That made me think how easy it was to get from here to France or Belgium and vice versa. Commit a robbery here and you can be in Europe before the alarm's raised so any road blocks are just wasting time and petrol. I began to wonder if the reason we still have no handle for the peterman, despite all our work and the information we've received, is because he's a foreigner who opened the safe and then skipped out of the country on Eurostar.

'As Quale was lying, fatally wounded, in the car park, he tried to say something. Mullins could only suggest "fog". What if Quale had heard the peterman speak and he did so in French and Quale wasn't trying to say fog, but *frog*?'

McGill spoke slowly. 'There are times when an unexpected moment of imagination is worth weeks of hard work. We'll get tapes from the CCTV security cameras covering the train on the relevant date and through Interpol ask France to examine every frame for the sight of a known, expert safecracker. The Sûreté won't welcome spending so much time and effort for the force of another country, but they owe us one. When we have the tapes, get on to the Interpol clearing house at Scotland Yard and ask them to forward the request.'

Nineteen

Weeks of unrewarding work had left Warren tired and suffering from a bitter sense of angry failure. He was checking the night duty list when the phone rang.

'Winthrop here, Interpol. With regard to your request to the French to identify known criminals travelling on Eurostar. Monsieur Bassonaud reports that after an inordinate, gruelling, eye-straining time spent examining tapes – he doesn't believe in quiet understatement – Jacques Citon, a heavy with plenty of form, was identified on tape eight; that's early morning, the sixteenth of September.'

'What about the peterman?'

'No sign of one, but it seems the tapes were in poor condition so they cannot say a known one was not aboard the train.'

'Shit!'

'The usual kind of break! They want to know if you're requesting any further action?'

'I'll get back on to you about that after I've had a word with the brass.' Warren said goodbye, replaced the receiver, dialled the hotel at which McGill was staying.

'What the hell is it this time?' was the welcome.

Warren repeated what he had been told.

'Bloody typical to use tapes which should have been replaced weeks before.'

'They want to know if we're requesting any further action?'

'You told them, of course we bloody do.'

'I said I'd find out from you before answering.'

'It didn't occur to you that this Frenchman should be

questioned and his place searched for anything incriminating?'

'Of course it did, but—'

'Get back to them and tell them what to do.' McGill cut the connection.

Winthrop phoned again the following evening. 'The French police searched the flat where Citon is living with – to repeat their description – "a hot piece". They found a number of loose English fifty-pound bank notes. Dirty clothes carried fragments of brick and they've bagged these along with a pair of gloves which carry stains which they suggest be analyzed. He was accused of burglary and murder, swore he'd never been in England and predictably claimed the picture of him on the tape was a fake.

'The French are asking if there's a chance of proving the money came from the supermarket's safe and if you've any information which will help confirm his guilt.

'That's how things stand at the moment. The French will continue to question Citon, but describe him as tough and without solid proof to tie him down, they doubt he'll give anything away.'

After that call was over, he again dialled McGill's hotel and asked to speak to him There was a long pause before contact was made. 'Sorry to break into your dinner, sir . . .'

'So am I.'

'I've just heard from the French again and I reckoned you'd want to know the news right away.'

'What is it?'

Warren detailed the facts he had been told.

'Not definite enough.'

'Time and date fit the break-in and murder.'

'What is the chance of proving the money came from the safe in the supermarket?'

'I haven't yet evaluated that.'

'Why not?'

'Only just been given the information, sir.'

'You couldn't start things moving before you interrupted my meal?'

If he had done so, Warren was certain he would have been criticized for acting without authority. The frustration of failure was feeding the chief superintendent's aggressive authority – and his colleagues were bearing the brunt of it.

Harmsworth looked up from his desk in the supermarket office as Chappell entered. 'Not again,' he said bitterly.

'Won't hold you up for more than a minute.'

'That was what I was told before. So I suppose I'll still be here when the wife's ready to serve the meal.'

With a casual ease which almost robbed the act of rudeness, Chappell sat on the edge of the desk. 'We're wondering if you can identify the money that was stolen?'

'Is that a serious question? With all the hundreds of notes which come in on a Sunday, you expect me to look at a fiver and say that was one of ours?'

'What about higher denominations?'

'People use tens and twenties like ten bob was spent when I was a kid.'

'And fifties?'

'Not so popular.'

'They're the ones of most interest. You noted their numbers?'

'Give me a break.'

'Do you keep any written record?'

'Look, we close on Sunday and I bundle up the notes in their separate denominations so there can be a quick confirmation of totals as they're handed over for the collection by the security people on Monday.'

'You note the totals of each denomination.'

'Of course.'

'And you keep Sunday's take separate from Monday's?'

'Yes.'

'Then you can tell me how many fifties you handled on the Sunday.'

'What's the point?'

'Leave it to us to find that out.'

Harmsworth muttered as he stood and crossed to one of the filing cabinets, pulled open the third drawer down, searched amongst the papers and files. 'Thanks to a temporary secretary who's in the glow of a recent engagement, it's a case of "ceaseless turmoil seething".'

'How's that?'

'In Xanadu.'

'What's that when it's at home?'

'You are not a poetry lover.'

'Don't mind a limerick with a bit of spice.'

Harmsworth finally found what he wanted, carried the folder to the desk, sat, opened the folder and brought out a form which he read. 'Twenty-seven.'

'Fifties?'

'That's what you asked.'

'Must be more money around than I ever see. They would have been in a separate bundle?'

'Yes.'

'Was there a wrapper?'

'Had to be, didn't there?'

'What was it like?'

'Same as on the others.'

'What were the others like and don't bother to tell me they were the same as on the fifties.'

'Plain white,' Harmsworth said resentfully.

'There was nothing on it denoting the notes came from here?'

'Wouldn't have been plain, then, would it?'

'You didn't write on it to record how many notes were in the bundle?'

There was a pause. 'I did, yes.'

'So they weren't completely plain.'

Silence.

'Do you write in pencil or pen?'

'Ballpoint.'

'Blue, red, green, or what?'

'Black.'

'Exactly whereabouts?'

'Top right-hand corner.'

'What about the seven? Did you put a stroke across the shank, like they do on the Continent?'

'No.'

'That's it, then.'

'You wouldn't like to know if I put a tilde above the two?'

'Do you?'

'No.'

'Then I wouldn't.' Chappell slid off the desk.

Warren phoned Interpol. 'We do have a further request for the French police in connection with Jacques Citon.'

'That'll make their day.'

'Shouldn't strain them too hard. Was there a wrapper around any of the bundles of notes? If not, would they search the flat to see if they can find a wrapper that had been torn open. If so, would they describe any writing or figures on the wrapper.'

It had become the custom once a month, at no set date but when all were free, for Gregg and Wendy, Guinevere and Lodge to meet at the Old Chestnut to have drinks and a meal, Dutch. It was a custom Wendy would have liked to bring to an end, but made no attempt to do so because Gregg enjoyed Lodge's company.

The Old Chestnut was one of the few public houses to escape gentrification; no thematic decoration deprived the bar of its louche ambience of heavily beamed ceiling with written comments – inane, amusing, not to be read by maiden aunts – stuck on the plaster between beams; time- and smoke-darkened walls; sanded floor; and stained painting of a well-endowed young woman stepping into a bath which had been presented to the bar by an indigent painter who had committed suicide soon after finishing it.

In the bar there were round windows through which, in

daylight, could be seen part of the village and, since the land sloped away, the fields and woods beyond. Leading off the bar was a small room in which, on four days of the week, a ploughman's supper was served. The name of the meal was the corruption of a myth, but the food was good.

They sat at one of the tables and, since only three other people were present, could talk without raising their voices. Gregg checked what they wanted to drink, went out and across to the bar to order, asked for the slate on which was written the menu. He carried glasses and slate back to their table.

Conversation was general until Guinevere spoke to Wendy. 'You're wearing a new ring!'

'Sharp of you to notice.'

'Do let me look at it.'

Reluctantly, Wendy held out her hand.

'It's very . . . interesting,' Guinevere said as she lightly held Wendy's hand to view the ring. 'And so attractive! How did you manage to find it?'

'Andy gave it to me.'

'Lucky you! . . . What is it?'

'A scarab.'

'A what?'

'A beetle which the ancient Egyptians honoured,' Gregg said. 'It's a relative of the dung beetle.'

'Oh!' She released Wendy's hand.

The landlord's wife came up to the table and asked them if they were ready to order their meals.

Gregg followed Lodge's car out on to the road, turned right.

'You're impossible,' Wendy said.

'Why?'

'Telling Guinevere that a scarab was related to the dung beetle.'

'It's true.'

'You knew how repulsive she'd find the thought of touching something connected to dung. She'll wash her hands five times over as soon as she gets home.'

'And congratulate herself on wearing a brooch ten times as valuable.'

'My ring is worth a hundred times more to me than that brooch means to her. And will you please drive home as quickly as you can because junior's making himself felt.'

Twenty

The white-clad forensic team finished their work and as a PC removed the tape which had surrounded the car park, the sergeant crossed to where McGill waited.

'That's it, sir. Nothing to report. Perhaps we'll have better luck inside.'

'Then what's holding you back from finding out?'

And up yours, the sergeant silently said as he walked away. As he approached the waiting constables, Harmsworth hurried across to speak to him. 'Is the car park at last opening?'

'Yes.'

'We've been losing custom with it closed. Nowhere for customers to park. The takings will be down and I'll have to make a full report to headquarters.'

'At least you'll be alive to make it.'

'How's that?'

'Forget it.'

'Someone said you're going to search the offices now?'

'That's right.'

'But I've a mass of work to get up to date . . .'

'If you want a quiet life, Mr Harmsworth, try not to have another copper killed here.'

'There's no call to speak like that!'

'A matter of opinion.'

The search of the office complex was completed three hours later. A cardboard box was filled with plastic bags, in each of which was an item to be examined in the laboratory, but none of the searchers was confident that any of them would prove to be of significance.

*   *   *

Warren knocked, entered Horton's room. 'France has just been through again, sir. They searched the flat once more and came across a torn wrapper under a bed. On it, written in black, are the figures two and seven. No continental sideways dash on the seven.'

'Then we can say the money which Citon had in his room was from the supermarket.'

'Provided Harmsworth identifies his own writing.'

'You need proof that water is wet? Get back on to them and say we can offer proof that Citon was mixed up in the robbery and murder. That will help them put the pressure on Citon and make him squeal . . . For the first time we can see a crack in the case.'

'Yes, sir.' Warren spoke dully.

'You're thinking there's not going to be room for celebration when it opens right out?'

'Shouldn't feel that way, I know. We have to land Quale's murderer. But it's bitter to recognize information was probably sold.'

'You still find room for doubt?'

'I try to, sir.'

On Friday evening, Warren was hoping he might at last be able to leave the office early – or at least on time – when the phone rang.

'Winthrop here. Frenchland reports that faced with the threat of a murder charge, Citon talked. He's a thug, but not stupid, and when he was being approached, wanted to know the pros and cons of working in England. No problem, he was told. The information to make things simple was coming from the English police – supplied by a detective.

'Ponchet was the peterman. Smart as they come. But he'd been a crazy idiot when he'd stuck his knife into the English policeman. Citon swore he had had nothing to do with that. Given the chance, he would have knocked the knife out of Ponchet's hand. Murder a copper and the sky fell before they'd give up the hunt, he said. Refused to name the third man.'

Warren thanked the other, replaced the phone. He felt mentally sick. Recently, he had been forced to accept the strong probability there was a traitor within the force, yet still he had hoped something would prove this was false. Now there could be no more illogical, wishful hope. There was a traitor in the CID.

He phoned Horton who was down in Nessden, infuriating the local coppers with his demand that some areas around the supermarket be searched yet again. 'Sir, France has been on again. Citon admits being on the supermarket job and names Ponchet the peterman. They had information from an English detective which had made the job at Murray's Superstore easy.'

Horton swore.

'Will you tell the chief super, sir?'

'You will.' Horton closed the contact.

Warren swore.

McGill paced the floor of the detective inspector's room. 'If you'd reported your suspicions of Gregg when you should, we'd not have ended up like this. His computer could have been checked.'

'Sir, there was no certainty. There's been none until now,' Horton replied.

'It needed Quale's death to convince you to look for it?'

'That's not fair.'

'It's fact.' McGill came to a stop. 'You told Gregg eight thirty?'

'Yes.'

McGill stared through the window at the road below as if to catch a sight of the missing man. 'Then where the hell is he? Heard the news and decided to do a runner?'

A knock on the door proved otherwise. Gregg entered.

'Half past eight does not mean a quarter to nine.'

'No, sir. The traffic—'

'Should have been allowed for.'

McGill returned to his seat. 'Am I correct you have guaranteed that the level of security of your work is so good

there is no chance that a single word of any report which
you make can escape?'

'Yes, sir.' Gregg had not been asked to sit. Senior officers seemed to consider this underlined their superiority.
Perhaps they forgot it meant they had to look up to their
juniors.

'You now confirm there is no way in which information
from one of your reports could accidentally be leaked?'

'Why are you asking, sir?'

'You will answer questions, not ask them.'

'There is no way unless one of the house owners to whom
a copy of the report has been given is stupid enough to pass
on some of the information.'

'We can ignore that possibility.'

'Do you know if anyone—'

'You do not understand English? You surveyed Querry
Brade on the' – he looked down at a sheet of paper – 'the
first of June?'

'I think so, but I'd have to confirm the date, sir.'

'Your report made it very clear that the existing security
was totally inadequate if a sharp team decided to make a
raid. Your description of what was lacking or what security gear was virtually useless went into great detail. You
recommended the immediate installation of an extensive,
sophisticated system, one that would make any attempted
robbery very difficult even for the experts. Five days later,
there was a robbery and valuable jewellery was stolen. Does
that say anything to you?'

'Only that the Irwins were very unlucky.'

'It doesn't puzzle you why the robbery took place in the
interval between your making the survey and the time when
a far better security system would be in operation?'

'I don't think so.'

'You see no connection?'

'Only a coincidence.'

'On Friday the thirteenth of June, you surveyed Murray's
Superstore in Nessden. You learned that the electricity
supply to the store and the offices were on different circuits

and both entered the building at a potentially vulnerable point. In your report, you wrote it was necessary that the lead to the security system be introduced into the building in a far more secure position. On Sunday the sixteenth of September, the supermarket was robbed. Do you know the details of how the building was entered without activating the alarm system?'

'The cable was cut.'

'By men who knew where the cable went.'

'The course of it was probably traced through a current-recording instrument.'

'When the cable was underground as far as the wall and then embedded in the wall?'

'I imagine there are instruments sufficiently sensitive to do that.'

'That the villains knew which cable fed the security system is obvious since only the one cable was cut. That they knew it was reached through brickwork is obvious since they arrived with brick-dissolving acid. In other words, they knew exactly how and where to break into the super-market. How do you explain that?'

'I can't, sir.'

'So we have two security surveys which detailed how any defences could be circumvented; then those defences breached.'

'It has to be coincidence.'

'I am tempted to paraphrase. To suffer one coincidence is normal; to suffer two in quick succession is discarnate. PC Quale was murdered because information had been fed to the villains. I will find out who fed it and he will be charged with being an accessory before the fact to murder and will then be banged up for as many years as he has left.'

'Are you accusing me of having passed on information?'

'Did you?'

'I did not.'

'The French have identified the peterman, Ponchet, and the heavy, Citon. Faced with being charged with murder,

Citon sang. They had full information on the security at
the store. This was provided by an English detective. At
Nessden, Ponchet panicked when approached by Quale and
murdered him. They returned to Paris on Eurostar.'

There was a long silence.

'If there's the slightest truth . . .' Gregg began.

'You have just heard the truth.'

'The information can't have come from CID.'

'Citon was definite. The information was guaranteed gold
because it came direct from a detective. Who here, by your
own evidence, were the only persons in a position to be
able to sell security information on the two buildings?'

'It's ridiculous.'

'Who?'

'But—'

'You find the question difficult to answer? Then I will
answer it for you. Only Sergeant Warren and Inspector
Horton, who read the report, and you. Do you accuse
Inspector Horton or Sergeant Warren of selling the information?'

'Of course not.'

'That leaves only you.'

'It's absurd.'

'It is logic.'

'It has to be—' He stopped.

'A mistake?'

'Someone else.'

'You have never stopped telling me CID was a team and
therefore could not harbour a traitor.'

'I have never sold information.'

'Information has been sold.'

'You've no proof,' Gregg said wildly.

'Proof, no, only strong assumptions. Which is why I am
not justified in suspending you. However, you are no longer
security officer and Sergeant Warren will make certain you
have nothing to do with any case which might provide you
with a further opportunity of selling sensitive information.'

'Under English law, a man is innocent until proven guilty.'

'But a guilty man is not presumed innocent.'

Moments later, Gregg entered the general room, visibly shaken. Lodge said, 'Good God, have you just had a heart attack and died?'

Gregg sat at his desk.

'What the hell's up? Has something happened to Wendy?'

'No.'

'So what's the catastrophe?'

'They're accusing me of being responsible for the murder of Quale.'

'Doing what? Are you sure you know what you're saying?'

'Yes.'

'But that accusation has to be nonsense.'

'Not to them.'

'Haven't the French identified the couple who did the supermarket job?'

'Yes.'

'Then you're talking balls. They've nailed the bastards who knifed Quale.'

'They accuse me of being an accessory before the fact.'

'Who's accusing you?'

'McGill and the DI.'

'Why?'

'One of the French villains has confessed. The jobs were carried out using information sold to them by CID here.'

'Christ!'

Gregg was too confused by his own problems to note there was fear as well as surprise in Lodge's exclamation. 'And I did the selling. It had to be me because that's logical. I've told him often enough that my security is total so no one else, apart from Warren and Horton, knew what was in my report. They don't come into the frame, so that leaves me.'

Lodge spoke with relief. 'They can't judge you're a bloke who wouldn't act the traitor even if you were offered a million?'

'Obviously not.'

'The break-ins following your reports have to be coincidences.'

'Not when the French say they were sold information. I'm thrown off security. And McGill is going to bust a gut to see me charged and convicted.'

'You're suspended from duty?'

'No.'

'Then you're panicking unnecessarily because surely you would have been if they were certain?'

'He hasn't enough proof yet to charge me.'

'What a bloody awful situation for you. How can I help?'

'Don't get mixed up in this quagmire.'

'You think that after being friends for all the years, I'm just going to sit back if there is anything I can do?'

'If there were, I'd ask. But how can one fight shadows?'

'By switching off the light that's making them.'

'Where's the switch?'

Lodge did not answer.

Lodge crossed the car park to Chappell's car, spoke through the opened window. 'Have you heard?'

'Depends what I'm supposed to have been listening to.'

'Andy's been thrown off security.'

'Who's told you that one? He knows the job backwards and had a verbal commendation not long ago. The guv'nor hands them out like they were gold sovereigns.'

'The sarge told me. Said one of us will be taking over.'

'Then some idiot up at county HQ must have decided in the name of broadening experience to move people from what they are best qualified to do.'

'The way he was talking made me think something serious was going on. Never heard him so bitter.'

'Something like what?'

'I don't know. Unless . . . Andy was called into the interview room by the super and Horton. He spent a long time there.'

'Maybe one of his surveys has gone sour.'

'I suppose you could say, two of them have.'

'Maybe, but that's through no fault of his.'

'You don't think . . .'

'What don't I think?'

'That rumour could be half right for once.'

'What rumour? What the hell are you saying?'

'It's now been confirmed information was sold by someone in CID. The super hasn't called you in today, has he?'

'No.'

'Me neither. Only Andy.'

'So?'

'Just seems it maybe could be significant.'

'You're saying they suspect him?'

'Not saying anything. Best not to talk about it or people might start getting the wrong idea.'

'You think I'm a loudmouth?'

You always have been, Lodge silently answered.

'These dates are good,' Guinevere said.

Lodge watched her pluck another off its stem. He wondered how she kept her figure when at times she ate extravagantly. He wondered at much greater length how her body could be as addictive as a class-A drug. 'Will you do something for me, love?'

'Don't say that. It's so common.'

'Sorry. Will you do something for me?' he asked a second time.

'What?'

'If you're ever asked, say you have met Aunt Sally several times.'

'Sarah. Sally is a pet name and sounds so ordinary.'

'Then say you have met Aunt Sarah.'

'But I haven't, so why should I say I have?'

'And explain it was Aunt Sarah who gave me the money to buy your brooch.'

'Who'll want to know that?' She ate another date.

'Will you?'

'Why should I?'

'It would help me tremendously.'

'You aren't making sense. Saying I've done what I haven't will help you?'

'I'd be very grateful.'

'Why?'

'Never mind. Incidentally, I was passing the travel agent's and had a look through the window. They're advertising a special cruise in December.'

'To the Isle of Man?'

'Three weeks and visiting the Azores, Antigua, St Kitts, and I can't remember where else in the West Indies, Madeira, and finally Vigo in Spain.'

'Some people can enjoy life, unlike me.'

'Like you.'

She had been about to eat another date; she held it in front of her mouth. 'Is that supposed to be funny?'

'No.'

'Just bloody. While they'll be having fun in all those places, I'll be sitting here, nothing to do, nowhere to go because you can't afford it.'

'I know how upset you've been over not being able to go to Jamaica . . .'

'No, you don't. You won't try to understand how shaming it is to hear Cynthia boasting about the wonderful time she's going to have.'

'It's because I understand that I decided I had to make things up to you. I phoned Aunt Sarah before lunch. She told me how kind it was of me to keep in touch with an old woman. I said it was a pleasure, not a burden, and that pleased her. She'd been wondering what to give me for my birthday, couldn't think of anything sensible, and would I mind if she gave me some money to buy what I wanted even if, in her day, it was not polite to give money. I told her she was far too kind to me . . .'

'That was bloody stupid. Likely to make her think twice.'

'It pleases old people to be told they're too generous; makes them feel noble. She wanted to know what I'd most like. I said to take you on a cruise to cheer you up after being so depressed by the death of your father and if she was kind enough to give me something, I'd put it towards a cruise for you. She said you wouldn't want to be on your own and she'd give me enough to pay for us both to go and it would give her tremendous pleasure to know she was helping you.'

'She really meant that?'

'I'm sure she did.'

She stared into the future.

'I'll give you a photograph so that you can describe her.'

'Who?'

'My aunt.'

'Why?'

'You've got to understand.'

'A genius couldn't!'

'Someone may come along and dispute she is my aunt.'

'How can they?'

'Darling, please do as I ask or I maybe could be in trouble.'

'It's all so stupid, me saying I've met your aunt and you wanting me to look at a photograph so I can describe what she looks like. I'm not going to do it.'

Fear of what her refusal could mean caused him to shout. 'You goddamn selfish bitch!' He waited for her venomous reply.

'Did I marry a man after all?' she said in astonishment.

Wendy kissed Gregg, stepped back and studied his face. 'Something's terribly wrong.'

'Why think that?'

'Because I'm married to you. What is it?'

'Let's go through.'

They went into the sitting room, sat.

'What kind of a day has junior allowed you to have?' he asked.

'Never mind me. What has happened to you?'

'The two men who committed the robbery at the supermarket and murdered Quale have been identified by the French police.'

'Surely that's great?'

'It would be if they didn't claim they'd had full information from CID on the security set-up.'

'That's not possible, is it?'

'It's fact.'

'It can't be.'

'McGill questioned me because he's convinced I'm the
one who sold the information about the security at Querry
Brade to the English villains and at the supermarket to
French villains.'

'You told him that was utterly absurd?'

'I tried to, but he wasn't listening. Only three people
were in a position to sell the information – Horton, Warren,
and me. That leaves me out in the cold.'

'How can he begin to think you'd do such a thing?'

'Circumstantial evidence does seem to point to me.'

'Then it's totally wrong.'

'He's stripped me of being security officer.'

'Can he be so stupidly blind?'

'He'd tell you he accepts facts.'

'You wouldn't sell information to save your life! They
ought to have the sense to understand that. Is it because
you're only a DC Plod and they're higher rank? Only PC
Plod could be crooked?'

'That's not how people of their rank think.'

'You've got to make them understand. Tell them you may
be only a DC, but you're just as honest as them . . .' She
stopped, turned her head away.

He got up from his chair, crossed to sit on the settee, put
his arm around her. 'It'll sort itself out.'

'You think that? Is that why you arrived home looking
like a beaten puppy?'

'If I'm innocent, they can't prove I'm guilty.'

'When they're so certain?'

'Thinking is different from proving.'

After a while, she said, 'What happens?'

'I suppose they'll start searching for signs of high
spending on my part – does my bank account have too
much money in it, that sort of thing.'

'Then all they have to do is see how little is there.'

'They'll expect off-shore accounts, hidden from view.'

'And they won't find those. So they'll be forced to admit they're wrong.'

'A negative won't be a positive. The lack of finding any dicey account won't convince them. If one knows the right name, pays a percentage, cash will be transferred to an off-shore account where there's no agreement for mutual disclosure of information.'

'You . . . you're beginning to worry me.'

'You've got to understand what can happen. Like questioning you and searching the house.'

'They'll do that?'

'A policeman was killed during the robbery and that took place because information on security had been sold. The seller is guilty of being an accessory before the fact. They believe that man was me, so they'll never stop trying to gather the evidence to land me.'

She pressed closer to him, junior kicking away between them.

Twenty-One

Guinevere had gone to bed; Lodge remained in the sitting room. When Gregg had told him it was certain the information had come from CID, he had been shocked. Gregg might be the obvious suspect, but would not be charged before the other members of CID were questioned and their backgrounds closely examined in order to eliminate them. Spending money was always incriminating. He had recognized that from the start, back when his extra money came merely from accepting bribes. That was why he had invented Aunt Sarah/Sally. She would explain how he was able to provide Guinevere with more luxury than his income permitted. Until Quale had been murdered, there had been no reason to fear the deception might be uncovered. Then, everything had blown up and he had had to be prepared to find a way of corroborating his non-existent aunt's existence. He had tried to persuade Guinevere to support him by claiming she had met Aunt Sarah many times and his aunt was the source of the extra money, but, ever self-centred, she had refused. Panicking, he had offered the cruise to persuade her, ignoring the consequences of doing so. Now, he had to accept there was no way in which they could spend thousands of pounds since to do so must risk exposing the deception. The cruise had to be cancelled. Guinevere would be furious . . . Yet he could not tell her now, not when to do so would immediately deprive him of what his mind and body demanded. Later . . .

'Aren't you coming up to bed?' she called out. 'Not in a hurry for once?'

There was the bitter, unwelcome thought that this might

be the last time for a very long while since her resentment was never short-lived. Halfway up the stairs, he enjoyed a moment of inspiration. His innocence lay in engineering another man's guilt.

On Sunday, Lodge knocked on the DI's door. There was a shout for him to enter.

Horton looked up. 'Well?' He did not try to sound pleasant. McGill was making his life hell.

Lodge stood in front of the desk. 'I thought I ought to have a word with you, sir.'

'Do I have to wait until tomorrow to know what about?'

'It's very difficult . . .'

'Then bugger off until you find it easier.'

'Andy's a friend of very long standing. I mean, we were at training college together . . .'

'I don't give a damn if you shared dummies in a cot. What the hell is all this about?'

'I don't like to suggest . . . especially as it may be sheer nonsense.'

'So far, everything you've said is nonsense.'

'I . . . I may have some information.'

'Regarding Gregg?'

'Yes, sir.'

'Well?

'I don't want you to think . . .'

'When you explain what your information is, I might be able to start thinking.'

'My maiden aunt, who lives just outside Liverpool, in a place called Benarden . . .'

'I am uninterested in the distribution of your family.'

'Of course. But the reason for mentioning her is that she's wealthy and frequently sends me quite large sums of money; as she says, I can get more fun out of it than she can because she's not very fit . . .'

'I am equally uninterested in their health.'

'But you see, sir, not long ago I bought my wife a brooch with money my aunt had just given me – Guinevere had fallen in love with it the moment she saw it in the jeweller's window – and she wore it to a dinner we had with the Greggs. Wendy was rather . . . *envious* is perhaps the right, if rather critical, word. You know how women are with jewellery. And I suppose it was that envy which is why, when we were having a meal at a pub some time later, she made a point of showing Guinevere a ring her husband had just bought her.'

'What kind of a ring?'

'A scarab one.'

'Was that after the robbery at Querry?'

'Yes.'

'Anything more?'

'I am sure there's nothing wrong in his having bought the ring . . .'

'Then why bother to come here and tell me about it?'

'However distressful it has been to do so, sir, I realized it was my duty to mention it so that it can be shown to have no connection with the robbery.'

'Very well.'

Lodge left. Now, should the purchase of the brooch become known, his mentioning it before he had to explain how he could afford it must add verisimilitude to his evidence.

'What do you know about scarab rings?' McGill asked, as he paced the floor in the DI's room.

Was he a keep-fit fanatic, suffered cramp in his legs, or just restless? Horton wondered. 'Nothing, sir.'

'From Egypt, but I've no idea if they're expensive. Find out.'

On Tuesday, Gregg parked alongside the CID car, climbed out into the warmth of the returned sun and began to walk across to the entrance of divisional HQ. A PC approached. Occasionally they played an inexpert game of squash together, amused by their incompetence. 'Morning, Joe.'

The PC walked past him.

Just received a rocket from his sergeant, Gregg surmised.

There were those with rank who considered they were only doing their duty when they found fault.

Lodge was the only person in the CID room. Gregg said, 'I've a message from Wendy. She wants Guinevere to name a date when you can come for a meal.'

'We can't for the moment.'

The curt answer surprised Gregg. 'You sound as if something has gone wrong?'

'Work.'

'The computer's on strike again?'

There was no answer.

Gregg shrugged his shoulders, crossed to his desk on which was an unstamped letter with his name on it. He sat, opened it. Inside was a single sheet of paper on which, in capital letters, was written – SHIT DOESN'T STINK AS BADLY AS A COPPER THAT LEAKS.

He looked up and across at Lodge. 'D'you know what I've got here, Sid?'

'No.'

'Any idea who left it?'

'No.'

The door opened and Warren looked inside. He spoke to Gregg. 'Where the hell have you been all morning?'

'Driving here, Sarge.'

'In my room.' He left.

'If brevity is the soul of wit, there's been some very witty conversation this morning.'

Lodge continued to work.

Gregg went along the corridor and into Warren's room. 'Sarge . . .'

'Get down to Hatchby, the clothing store in Elsey Street. Breaking and entering during the night.'

'Is that it?'

'Yes.'

'I'm wondering why everyone has started speaking in shorthand and why someone thought it amusing to leave a message on my desk suggesting I suffer from acute BO?'

'Don't bother to sound surprised.'

'Not surprised. Bewildered.'

'The information sold came from CID.'

'That's a load of balls.'

'It's confirmed.'

'I still don't believe it.'

'People are thinking it has a lot to do with you.'

'Why?'

'You're suddenly spending money like your name's Bill Gates.'

'What are you talking about?'

'You'll bloody soon find out.'

Horton reported to McGill, who had finally been provided with a temporary office. 'We've been on to a couple of jewellers, sir. Scarab rings come from Egypt; genuine ones from ancient Egypt. They were quite the rage back in the beginning of last century, but are far less popular now. One of the jewellers thinks he can probably find a gold one from the Middle Kingdom – whenever that was – for three thousand. They are still being made and it's easy to be taken for a ride, so one needs the judgment of an expert before buying.'

'Did Lodge describe the ring Mrs Gregg was wearing?'

'No.'

'So we could be dealing with a ring that's valuable or not worth all that much?'

'It seems to be that way.'

'We need to find out how much it cost and how it was paid for. We'll interview Gregg tomorrow morning, ten o'clock.'

'Right, sir.'

'And if we find cause, I want a search made of his house.'

'On a warrant?'

'If he's innocent and has any sense, he'll not demand one.'

McGill's office, demanded by him and finally provided, had been a store room. It had been cleared up, but too quickly.

The window still showed dust trails; a cobweb hung from the ceiling at one corner. The furniture would have delighted a rag-and-bone man. The table had come from the conference room where it had been acting as sideboard and suffered considerable marking; the three chairs had come from different rooms and were of different designs; the springs of the adjustable desk lamp were weak so that it had to be constantly adjusted; the overhead light was unshaded; there was no carpet and the linoleum was worn. However, a new paper basket had been brought up from stores.

McGill and Horton sat on one side of the table, Gregg the other.

'Is there anything more you have to say about your survey of Murray's Superstore?'

'No, sir.'

'You deny you sold information concerning the security which enabled the robbery to be readily carried out?'

'Yes, sir.'

'You deny you were guilty of implication in PC Quale's death?'

'Yes, sir.'

'Selling means there has been a payment. How much would you think the seller of the information received in this case and that of Querry Brade?'

'I've no idea.'

'You'd agree it must have been a substantial sum since the risks to the informer who chose whom to inform were great, the benefits to the villains, very great?'

'I suppose so.'

'How substantial?'

'I've already said, I have no idea.'

'Certainly, the seller would be able to allow himself a luxury, or two. What would be your choice of a luxury?'

'The question is meaningless.'

'Why?'

'I repeat, I have never sold information to anyone.'

'You have not recently bought a new car – a BMW or a Jaguar, for instance?'

'My Ford Fiesta was bought second-hand two years ago.'

'A large flat-screen television?'

'You imagine I've just refurbished our house?'

'I should like to know if you have.'

'Whatever I answer, you won't believe me.'

'What makes you say that?'

'I'm not a fool. Your questions make it all too clear what you think.'

'We will be asking every member of CID the same questions.'

'With the same hostility?'

'You are confusing hostility with our need to identify the traitor in CID as soon as possible.'

'You've convinced yourselves you're questioning him right now. No matter how often I swear I've never sold information, how many years I've served without putting up a black, or what kind of person I am, you've come to a conviction and are trying to bend the facts to warrant that.'

'For a DC, you have an unfortunate misconception of how a criminal investigation must be carried out. Your PC has been checked. It has only been active when the password was correctly entered. So information was not illegally gained from it.'

'I was in the best position to sell and since you can't find anyone else who fits the picture, I'm marked. Word's got around you're gunning for me and the lads think you wouldn't be doing that unless I was guilty, so now I'm the bastard responsible for Quale's death. They'd rather spend the day with a poxy ponce than me.'

'I am as intent on proving your innocence as your guilt.'

'And I'm the chief constable's honey-girl.'

'You do yourself no benefit by talking wildly.'

'Or by telling the truth.'

'Would you say you have recently been spending more money than you usually do?'

'No.'

'I believe your wife is pregnant. Have you not bought the essentials, such as cot, pram, clothes, and so on?'

'Some of them.'

'Then surely you have been spending considerably more than usual?'

'That's not what you were getting at.'

'Have you recently purchased jewellery for your wife?'

'No.'

'You have not bought her a scarab ring?'

'How the hell do you know about that?'

'Is it true?'

'Yes.'

'Yet you've just denied buying her any jewellery.'

'I don't call it jewellery.'

'Did you purchase it from a jeweller's?'

'Yes.'

'Then I suggest normal usage would call a ring bought in a jeweller's as jewellery. Is it gold?'

'Stone.'

'A stone ring?'

'The scarab is stone. The ring is gold.'

'How much did it cost?'

'Four hundred and fifty quid.'

'Would you not call that a considerable sum for a constable who has to buy all the necessaries his coming child will require in addition to the normal running costs of a home?'

'My wife has always wanted a scarab ring. I've been saving for a long time.'

'Out of your pay?'

'Yes.'

'You find your salary stretches much further than it does for most?'

'By skipping meals in the canteen and not joining the lads in a local boozer after work.'

'That would have called for very considerable self-sacrifice.'

'And you can't imagine me capable of that?'

'I am merely making an observation. How did you pay for the ring? By cheque or plastic?'

'Cash.'

'An unusually large sum in cash. But presumably, before paying, you drew it from wherever you deposit your salary – bank, building society?'

'I kept it in cash from the beginning.'

'Somewhat risky.'

'I had to keep it secret from my wife since she handles our financial matters to save me the bother.'

'Then she will not be able to confirm that you had possession of a sum in cash before the theft at Querry Brade?'

'Obviously not.'

'Unfortunate.'

'Only for someone who doesn't want to think. If I'd benefited from the two robberies, wouldn't I have bought a bloody big diamond ring?'

'Since you have told us your wife had long wanted a scarab ring, you were likely to earn her gratitude far more by buying that rather than a diamond one, which must immediately draw attention to your apparently new-found wealth.'

'You could twist an iron bar into a corkscrew.'

'In view of all the evidence, I am suspending you from duty until it becomes clear there is no danger in your continuing to work.'

Twenty-Two

'Why won't they believe you?' Wendy asked despairingly.

'Because a detective is trained to disbelieve an archangel,' Gregg replied.

She put her arm around his shoulder as they sat on the settee.

'I'm afraid they're likely to search the house.'

'Why?'

'To uncover the load of cash they think I might have hidden here.'

'If you had any, you'd have moved it the moment the trouble started because you'd know what could happen.'

'Moving actual cash in quantity is never easy if you don't want to deal with people who are waiting for a chance to steal it from you.'

After a moment, she said, 'They'll look everywhere in the house?'

'Yes.'

'Through all the clothes?'

'Yes.'

'It's horrid.'

'They'll be careful.'

'Have you forgotten what you told me about one search you were on?'

'I'm sorry, I don't remember.'

'When one of the PCs pulled out from a drawer a very skimpy pair of women's pants, he waved them around and said she was a real lady because she made it so easy for the men.'

'With Horton present, there'll be nothing like that. Anybody trying to be funny will be put on a charge.'

'But he can't stop them thinking that sort of a thing . . . They say you bought my ring with money you made from selling information and refuse to believe you had saved and saved to buy it?'

'They wouldn't accept that on my pay I could save anything since on top of living expenses, you are pregnant so we had to prepare for the arrival of junior.'

'Then what do they say about Sidney's buying that diamond brooch for Guinevere?'

'Why should they say anything?'

'Won't they want to know how he could possibly have afforded it?'

'First, his aunt paid for it; second, they probably don't know anything about it.'

'Then how did they learn about my ring?'

'I've no idea.'

'Someone must have told them.'

'I can't think who.'

'Then you're not thinking enough.'

'What are you getting at?'

'Shouldn't they be told about the brooch?'

'Why?'

'To find out where the money to buy it did come from.'

'We've been through that. It was from his aunt.'

'Have you ever met her?'

'No.'

'Then how do you know she exists?'

'How do I know anyone does? Maybe all of us – even you – exist only in the mind.'

'Please don't be condescending. I'm serious. How do you know Aunt Sarah exists if neither you nor I have ever met her?'

'He's told us about her often enough, shown us a photograph of her; she gives him money which she's hardly likely to do if she's not his aunt.'

'Does she?'

'What?'

'Give him money?'

'He won't find it in a field.'

'Suppose he invented Aunt Sarah in order to explain why he has far more money to spend than his known pay would allow?'

'You're really taking off!'

'Did he ever mention her when you first met?'

'I don't remember his doing so, but that hardly means she may not exist.'

'He's the kind of man who will always boast if there's reason and a rich relative would be almost as boast-worthy as a title. When did he first tell you about her?'

'I said, I haven't the faintest.'

'I'll bet it was after he met Guinevere.'

'Why?'

'Because if she was to stay interested in him, he had to feed her love of spending. So he invented a wealthy aunt as a way of explaining all the money he made illegally. You've always said there's a small fortune to be made on the streets by a crooked policeman; the tart who wants peace in which to work, the man who doesn't need a policeman around when he's selling stolen or smuggled goods in a pub.'

'I know you're trying to help, but this is crazy.'

'Is it?'

'After all the years we've known each other, you imagine he would sit back and watch me being unjustly accused and ostracized?'

'You're ignoring Guinevere again. If he confessed, he'd lose her once and for all; she'd never wait outside the prison gate for him. He wouldn't think twice about letting you go to hell to save her for himself.'

He stood, careless that he jerked her arm away from himself. 'You've never liked him; her, even less.'

'Can't you understand this isn't about like or dislike? I'm trying to save you by making you understand what could be the truth.'

'By branding my best friend a vicious coward?' He walked out of the room.

The front doorbell rang at 10.15. Wendy stood, went into the hall and along to the front door, comforting her stomach with her left hand. She opened the door to face Gregg, Horton, and two PCs.

Gregg stepped inside. 'They asked me to give permission for them to search the house. I gave it.'

'Why?' she demanded angrily.

'If I had refused, they'd have obtained a search warrant which might have resulted in publicity.'

Horton said, 'I'm sorry, Mrs Gregg, for the necessity—'

'No, you're not. You're incapable of feeling sorry about what you're doing. Driving Andy into depression because you won't listen to him, accusing him when he's done nothing, treating him like a criminal.'

'I fear we have to do our job, however much distress it causes, however much we dislike doing it.'

'Nothing could give you more pleasure.'

Gregg spoke. 'Come on back into the room, love.'

'No. They're not going up to our bedroom to make filthy jokes about me.'

He gently made her turn, move forward through the open doorway, into the sitting room.

'Go with them,' Horton ordered one of the PCs.

'Is that really necessary?' Gregg asked bitterly.

'You know the form.'

The PC, clearly embarrassed, followed them into the room.

They sat, close together on the settee. Gregg tried to comfort her, the PC stood by the window and resolutely stared out.

Wendy walked into divisional HQ at nine on Friday, came to a halt by the counter in the front reception.

The duty PC took his time to acknowledge her. 'Yes, Mrs Gregg?'

'I want to speak to Inspector Horton.'

'For what reason?'

'I will explain that to him.'

'Perhaps you would ring and make an appointment?'

'I want to see him now.'

The PC stepped back into the small office behind the counter. He did not lower his voice. 'The scumbag's wife wants a word with Inspector Horton, Sarge.'

Wendy wanted to cry.

'Tell him, then.'

The PC returned, used the internal phone to speak briefly, replaced the receiver. 'You can wait there.' He pointed.

She went into the small alcove and sat. On the glass-topped table were several out-of-date magazines and three up-to-date leaflets explaining how the police were continually improving their services to the public.

Time passed. Eventually the PC called out that the inspector would see her now; he made no effort to escort her to the DI's room.

Horton showed more manners than the PC had. He welcomed her pleasantly, tactfully asked how she was feeling, moved a chair on which he placed a cushion.

He settled. 'How can I help you, Mrs Gregg?'

'By believing my husband.'

His manner changed. 'It will be best if I say right away that I cannot discuss the case with you.'

'But I can discuss it with you. Andy has never done anything criminal in his life. He—'

'Please.'

'Why won't you listen? You've made your mind up and that's that? Hounding an innocent man doesn't matter?'

'I must ask you to leave.'

'I'll leave, but not before I tell you something. You believe Andy's guilty because he bought me a ring. That money came from saving; not eating as well as he should, not having a beer with his friends.'

Horton stood. 'I hope you will leave of your own accord, Mrs Gregg.'

'Not before you tell me why buying a scarab ring for four hundred and fifty pounds is suspicious, but buying a brooch for over two and a half thousand is not.'

Horton slowly sat. 'You are referring to the brooch Constable Lodge gave his wife?'

'You know about it?'

'Yes.'

'But still ignore it?'

'Constable Lodge informed me of the purchase and explained how he was able to make it.'

'I suppose he told you his rich aunt gave him the money?'

Horton did not answer.

'Are you so certain he has a rich aunt? Have you checked that she is not a cloak to hide how he really gained the money?'

'No.'

'Why not?'

'It has not been necessary to do so.'

'Because you're so convinced Andy is guilty? You refuse to try to uncover the truth because that would prove you've been wrong from the beginning. Your pride is so much more important than his innocence.'

Horton once more stood, crossed to the door, opened it and called out. A PC hurried up to him. 'Escort Mrs Gregg out of the station.'

The PC entered. 'Come on. Make it easy for yourself.'

She walked out, head held high even as bitter defeat speared her mind.

Gregg reported to Warren. 'I've spoken to Mrs Farnby about her missing moped. She's in a bit of a state and it took quite a time to calm her down sufficiently—'

'Just make your report.'

Gregg went to move a chair.

'Do it standing.'

'I had the whisper it was a couple of kids from the Raith Estate; brothers known for their thieving hands.'

'You questioned them?'

'They weren't at home and naturally no one was willing to suggest where they might be.'

'You couldn't be bothered to hunt around?'

'It was too small a job to spend much time on it. But if you want me—'

'I've had the guv'nor blasting my head off because of you,' Warren said angrily. 'Your wife called here earlier on.'

'Why?'

'To tell the guv'nor how to conduct the case.'

'She . . . she's been very upset, especially by the search of the house. So upset that as soon as it was over, she washed all her underclothes.'

'She accused Sidney Lodge of selling the information because he'd bought his wife an expensive brooch. Told him Sid doesn't have a rich aunt as he's always claiming.'

'I'm sorry, but like I said—'

'The guv'nor sends you a message. If you want to try and get out of the hole you've dug by falsely accusing someone else, would you have the guts to do that yourself?'

'You reckon I asked her to come here?'

Warren did not answer.

'I did something very stupid this morning,' Wendy said, as Gregg entered the hall from outside.

'So I learned.'

She hurried forward and hugged him as closely as her pregnancy allowed, seeking comfort. 'Will you ever forgive me?'

'No.'

'But I couldn't just sit here and do nothing while you—'

'I won't forgive you because there is nothing to forgive. You were trying to help me and it's not every wife would have the courage to face Horton.'

'I couldn't make him listen.'

'You did all you could.' He kissed her. He was glad she would probably never understand that challenging Horton as she had might well have hammered one more nail into his coffin.

Horton must now believe that he was trying to lay the guilt on Lodge.

Twenty-Three

As Guinevere crossed the road, Wendy briefly questioned whether she over-dressed to draw attention to herself or because she lacked the taste to dress elegantly.

'I thought it must be you,' Guinevere said. 'You didn't see me wave?'

'No.'

'Can't think why since you were looking in my direction. Where are you off to?'

'Marks and Spencer.'

'I bought some duck a l'orange there the other day and Sidney said how tasty it was; usually he can't be bothered to say anything. And all I had to do was pop it in the microwave . . . I'm feeling elevenish, so let's go along to the Lion and have coffee and a patisserie, or maybe the Bell as it's nearer and their patisseries are nicer, although the other people who are there are not.'

'I'm in a rush.'

'The other day, a doctor on television said one should never rush, no matter what the problem, because it causes stress. I'm stressed without rushing and must talk to someone or I'll have a stroke. Men! God, how I hate them!'

'You surprise me.'

'Always let you down. Come and have just a quick coffee?'

About to refuse again, Wendy checked the words. Guinevere would go on and on until only rudeness would bring a halt. 'All right, so long as we don't stay long.'

Coffee was served in the 'Petit Salon', which was

decorated in provincial snob style. Two of the waitresses were aging and slow; the third was young and indifferent.

They ordered.

'How's Andy?' Guinevere asked.

'All right.'

'It must be very difficult for him.'

'It is.'

'I simply can't think how anyone could possibly believe he'd do such a terrible thing. You must be so very worried.'

'I am, so perhaps we could talk about something else?'

'Of course. I mean, you don't want to be reminded that if your son's born when he is in . . . Oh dear! Sidney keeps telling me my tongue is too busy. Mind you, he doesn't *always* say that.' She giggled.

One of the slow waitresses brought them their order. As she walked away, Guinevere said, 'Would you mind if I have the chocolate éclair?'

'Go ahead.'

She had a mouthful of éclair. 'Sidney really is impossible. He promised to take me on a cruise.'

'Lucky you!'

'No, I'm not. I kept asking him if he'd booked so I could shut Cynthia up when she returns and starts boasting about her holiday in Jamaica. He started saying he didn't know if it was going to be possible after all and finally he told me his aunt had said maybe she wouldn't be able to help him. Of course, I said to get back on to the old bitch, butter her up, tell her how necessary the sea trip was for both of us. This morning he spoke to her again and she was in some sort of trouble and was sorry, but couldn't give him any more money now. So the cruise is off.'

'Just like a man! Gets you all excited and then walks away. Not that any of them actually do . . . If you don't want it, I'll have the last éclair. I wonder if it's praline?' She began to reach out, stopped as she stared at Wendy. 'Is something the matter?'

'No.'

'You're looking peculiar.'

'Junior kicked me.'

'Thank God I decided kids weren't for me.'

Wendy hurried into the house and called out. Gregg pulled open the door of the sitting room. 'Have the waters burst, do we need to rush to the hospital?'

'You're way ahead of schedule.'

'The way you came in and shouted had me panicking.'

'I've some news.'

'How bad?'

'Good. But I need to sit before I tell you what it is.'

They settled in the sitting room.

'I met Guinevere when I was out,' she said.

'And you call that good luck?'

'She told me Sidney had promised to take her on a cruise. Then he began to hum and haw and suggest his aunt might not be giving him enough money. This morning, he said she couldn't afford to give him anything so the cruise is off.'

He was silent.

'Don't you see what that means?'

'I think I understand what you think it means. Because of the trouble at work, it's a dangerous time to be spending. McGill's returned to county HQ, but Horton is just as smart and if he learns Sid is off on a luxury cruise, he will start asking questions about the rich aunt. But—'

'Don't give me more nonsense about Sidney being such a good friend, he'd always come to your aid. At the first sign of trouble, he'd run away.'

'It's so difficult . . .'

'Not for me. So I'm going to go and find out if he really does have a rich aunt.'

'In your condition?'

'As Guinevere had pleasure in pointing out, if nothing's done our son is likely to be born when you are in prison. You can't stop me doing everything possible to prevent that happening.'

'I won't try to.'

Her surprised bewilderment was obvious.

'First, though, tell me how you are going to trace his aunt?'

'Sidney knows where she lives.'

'And if she is fictitious, he certainly won't tell you. Nor will he if there is a woman posing as his aunt in order to pass money which appears to be legitimate.'

'Guinevere is so stupid, she'll tell me without realizing it . . .'

'If the aunt does not exist, Sidney will have told her nothing germane, in particular an address, for fear she unwittingly blabs.'

She spoke slowly, despondently. 'You're telling me there's no way of finding out.'

'No way for you.'

'Then . . .'

'But I could stand a chance.'

'You finally believe I'm right?'

'That you could be right because of the coincidence of the cancelled cruise at a time when spending heavily must draw attention to the source of the money.'

Life proceeded in a loop. Because Lodge had possibly betrayed their friendship, Gregg was about to try to betray it; if Lodge had lied to harm him, he was about to lie to try to harm Lodge.

'Yes?' Guinevere said over the phone.

'It's Andy.'

'This makes my day!'

'What about the night?'

'I'll find out when Sidney's on duty.'

For some reason – Wendy would have identified it – they often spoke to each other in jokingly suggestive terms. 'I've been suspended from duty. But you must know that.'

'I was absolutely shocked to hear it. How can they be so stupid? As I said to Sidney, one might as well suspect him as you.'

'Nice of you to say so. I'm ringing because a pal at HQ

had a call from Sidney's aunt. She has to speak to him because she's something very important to tell him about a trip and he'll want to know what that is as soon as possible.

'The PC who spoke to her was a sympathetic soul – some of the lads would have told her the station was not a message centre – and he asked her for her phone number so that Sidney could ring immediately he appeared. As she gave it, the wires started clicking and that, together with the difficulty of understanding her anyway because she must be an elderly woman with difficulty speaking clearly, meant he failed to catch what she said. As he was about to ask her to repeat it, she rang off.

'Like I said, the PC is the kind of bloke who goes out of his way to help others and because there was nothing more urgent on at the moment, he took the time to get on to me for help. I tried to get hold of Sidney, but couldn't, so I reckoned the best thing was to get in touch with you.' It was a weak, unlikely story, but he had, he hoped, helped to prevent her realizing that by seeding the thought in her mind the probability was that the call was to say she would give Lodge the money she had originally promised. 'What's the name of Sid's aunt?'

'Please, it's always Sidney.'

'You don't like diminutives?'

'Full size only.'

'No problem here . . . What is her name?'

'Sarah. Sarah Lingfield.'

'And her phone number?'

'I don't know it off-hand, but it'll be in the book. He told me to ring her if anything ever happened to him.'

'Would you look?'

'At what?'

He waited.

'It's very odd,' she said.

'No odder than most.'

'The phone number, you idiot. He's crossed it out.'

'So it's indecipherable?'

'Very nearly. There are pencil marks right across it.'

'Put the paper up against a light, back to front.'

'Your hobby?' After a while, she said, 'I can only just about read the first five numbers; the rest could be anything.'

'What are the five?'

She told him. He thanked her, promised to find out when was Lodge's next night duty, rang off.

He had the aunt's name and enough of her telephone number to ascertain in what area she lived. He would use his rank to get the telephone people to back-track the number and give him the address.

If Lodge had put his future at risk because of Guinevere, she might unknowingly be about to express her gratitude by ruining him.

Twenty-Four

The town of Myoe had maintained its old English name – without accents – despite several attempts to change it on the grounds that it was too open to mockery. Containing a small, but near perfectly preserved Norman cathedral, it had still not been accorded a charter, officially turning it into a city. The centre was partially Elizabethan and thanks to an unusually sympathetic local authority, this had not been desecrated by stores whose concept of beauty lay in cash registers.

The outskirts were a normal mixture of detached, semi detached, and terrace houses, small shops struggling to survive by offering better quality and service, and one garage.

No. 43, Abbot Road, was a greengrocer's. Gregg looked through the opened driving window of his car and swore. Guinevere must have read the telephone number incorrectly. Then he looked up at the name. Lingwood & Son. Perhaps she had muddled things, her mind not on what she was saying. Wood and field carried a similar connotation. There was only one way of finding out – clutch at a sodden straw. A car behind him hooted impatiently and he drove on until he found a parking space.

He walked back down the road, past small front gardens which were colourful, neglected or tarmacked to provide off-road parking. On the pavement outside Lingwood & Son, boxes of vegetables and fruit, mostly guaranteed to be locally grown and organic, were set out on stands. He entered the shop.

A blowsy woman, overalls stained, said, 'What would you like, love?'

'Is Mr Lingwood in?'

'Are you selling?'

'No. I'd just like a quick chat with him.'

She hesitated, finally said, 'He's in the office.' She pointed to the rear of the shop.

He walked past the counter and more boxes on stands, this time filled with tropical or semitropical fruit individually wrapped in tissue paper. The office was small, overfilled with filing cabinets, smelling of the strange sweetness which emanated from the tropical fruits outside.

Lingwood – round head, floppy ears, thinning hair, large brown eyes, crooked nose, thin mouth, stubbled chin – was talking angrily over the phone. He was being billed for three boxes and had only received two and it was no good trying to tell him he had had three . . . He did not look up, motioned with his hand to sit.

Gregg remained standing. He studied Lingwood's face, certain he had met him before, yet unable to recall when, where, or why. Not a recent meeting, for sure. Those ears must have earned him many a ragging in the playground . . .

'You'd have thought they wouldn't try that one on me. Think I can't count?' Lingwood said, as he replaced the receiver. 'So what's your problem? If you've a coldstore full of apples, I'm not buying . . .' For the first time, he looked directly at Gregg and his close-set eyes flicked away to focus on the open doorway.

For Gregg, it was a give-away. Criminals and detectives frequently developed the ability to identify an opponent on sight. The constantly searching eyes of the detective as he walked past people, the inability of a criminal to meet him eye-to-eye. 'Mr Lingwood?'

'You ain't local.'

His answer indirectly acknowledged what Gregg had already divined. 'No.'

'Then you ain't been told I run a straight business.'

'No.'

'There's not so much as a tomato I can't show you a receipt for.'

'You print your receipts on a private press?'

'You accusing me of something?'

'No.'

The answer perplexed Lingwood. 'Collecting insurance money?'

'No,' Gregg replied, sharply.

He began to fidget with the corner of a piece of paper. 'How long have you known Guinevere Lodge?'

The paper stilled. 'Who?'

'Hard of hearing?'

'Don't know the name.'

'So why should she want to ring you?'

'I tell you, I ain't never met the name.'

'But you have met her husband, Sidney Lodge.'

'What are you on about?'

'Finding out the reason why she was to ring you if there was any trouble for her husband.'

'Don't mean nothing to me. I've work to do so if you—'

'I've more questions to ask.'

'Then you'll answer them yourself.'

'You lease this place?'

After a moment, Lingwood said, 'No.'

'You own the building as well as the business?'

'Ain't nothing to do with you.'

'Where did the money come from?'

Lingwood was silent.

'You have a partner, don't you?'

'What if I do?'

'A non-working partner who receives a large share of the profits?'

Silence.

'Any good accountant will turn up the answers after looking through cash books, bank balances, cheque stubs, receipts.'

Silence.

'I'm guessing there will have been times when the profits of this business have been well above what normal trading would provide. And that's when your partner received large cheques which went legitimately into his bank. That's the way the scam has been working, isn't it?'

Silence.

'Of course, declared profits draw tax, but a clever man can arrange mythical purchases to match mythical sales to keep tax low.'

'Don't know what you're on about.'

'Try harder.'

'You lot won't let a man earn an honest living.'

'My definition of an honest living will be very different from yours.'

'You ain't got nothing on me.'

'Only that you have a direct link with a murder.'

Silence.

'You're willing to take the risk of having the facts dug out rather than volunteering them and receiving brownie points for being co-operative?'

Yet more silence.

Gregg shut the front door. 'How have things been with you?'

'The same,' Wendy replied. 'Have you been able to do something? Did you meet the so-called aunt? Did she tell you what was going on?'

'Let's go in and sit.'

As she settled on the settee in the sitting room, he said, 'I'll pour a lager and, before you ask, a small sherry for you.'

'It didn't go well, did it?'

'I learned who was at the telephone number. A greengrocer.'

'Not the aunt? And I so desperately hoped . . . Oh, God!'

'It's not all gloom and doom. When I spoke to the owner of the shop, we identified each other.'

'What's that mean?'

'He has been a criminal and almost certainly still is one, though in a different line of business from whatever it was before. The mention of Sidney threw him.'

'Then we're right?'

'Ex-criminals occasionally start leading blameless lives. He appears to be doing just that. But it's a thousand pounds to a penny, he isn't. Sidney must have bought the business through him and uses it to launder money. Books are kept, accounts will be in order, so on the face of things, the business is kosher.'

'If he's investigated, won't the truth come out?'

'Two big ifs. Can the local police be persuaded to carry out a full investigation, which means expensive accountants and business experts have to be called in, when it will be the case of another force? Will a thorough investigation expose the truth?'

'It must!'

'There can't be certainty.'

'It has to.'

'Right always prevails? If only.'

'Then what are you going to do?'

'Speak to the guv'nor. But will he take any notice of what I have to say? Will he presume I'm merely trying again to throw the guilt off my shoulders on to Sidney's?'

'Because . . . because of what I said to him?'

'Your visit won't have altered anything.' He spoke with a certainty he didn't feel.

Warren was leaving for the night as Gregg stepped out of his car.

'What do you want here?' Warren demanded roughly.

'A word with the guv'nor.'

'It still hasn't reached you that you're as welcome as reverse drainage?'

'I've important information.'

'Unimportant lies?'

'Facts.'

'What are they?'

'I'll tell him.'

'He's more likely to be ready to believe you than me?'

'That wouldn't be difficult.'

Warren walked on.

Gregg entered the building, went into the front room.

The duty sergeant watched him approach, his expression contemptuous. Gregg passed the counter, crossed to the stairs.

'It's no admittance, scumbag,' the sergeant called out.

He reached the fourth floor, went along the corridor to Horton's door, knocked, entered.

Horton was attending to a mountain of paperwork.

'I'd like a word, sir.'

'You have lost the right to enter the building as a serving officer.'

'And the right to prove my innocence?' He came to a stop in front of the desk. 'I set out to learn the name and address of Lodge's rich aunt. Took a bit of doing, but in the end I succeeded. Sarah Lingfield, 43 Abbot Road, Myoe. I also learned that Guinevere Lodge was to ring his aunt if there was ever any trouble for him. Seems odd. Trouble usually means fire, theft, sudden illness. Why call for help from far away when emergency help is close to hand? I drove up to find out what I could. The address proved to be that of a greengrocer, Lingwood and Son. Seemed there had to be a mistake since why would she ring a greengrocer for help?'

'What are you after with all this?'

'The truth. Lingwood denied knowing a Guinevere Lodge. Said I must have had the wrong phone number. I'd have accepted that if I hadn't sussed him as an ex-con. That's when things finally fell into place.

'Guinevere is Sidney's Achilles's heel. What she wants, she has to have. So he needed to find extra money. It's not difficult for a bent copper to do that if he's not greedy. But he was going to have to spend a lot on her, and so there would be the problem of being seen to live way above his income. He had to devise a money-laundering scheme. Lingwood is an ex-con. Through Sidney, he bought the greengrocer's in his name. The business seems to be run legit, almost certainly with all taxes paid. When black money rolls in, phantom purchases, sales, and profits are recorded. Money can now be paid to Sid in the name of his elderly, wealthy aunt and spent on Guinevere without causing questions. But the more she had, the more she wanted and eventually this meant bigger crimes – selling details of the security in Querry Brade and Murray's Superstore – and that's when things started to go wrong.

'The facts have to be hidden in the books of the green-grocer. Proving everything may take a little time—'

'Weeks, months, if he's as smart as you make him out to be. You think another force is going to waste time and money on your conjectures?'

'Yes, if you back the request.'

'I have no wish to commit professional hara-kiri.'

'You refuse to believe I'm right?'

Horton spoke contemptuously. 'After the Querry job, did you assure me there was no way in which anyone could break into the information on your computer?'

'Yes.'

'Then how could Lodge have gained knowledge of the information which you claim he sold?'

'I made a stupid mistake.'

'Yes. By cutting off an escape route through claiming security was complete.'

'By using the date Wendy's pregnancy was confirmed as the code.'

'My understanding of security is that numbers of anniversaries are never to be used.'

'If I would easily remember the code, there was no need to note it down – except in the sealed envelope in the station's safe. By using the date of confirmed pregnancy, I believed it was a number no one else could know or deduce.'

'Yet you are claiming Lodge could?'

'He had been at our wedding. He and Guinevere had dinner with us the day my wife was told by her doctor that her pregnancy was confirmed. She was so excited, it's inevitable she told the other two the news.'

'And you want me to believe Lodge would have remembered that date?'

'You must acknowledge the mind can work in odd ways.

Not very long ago, I forgot the date of an anniversary and that upset my wife, yet I have never forgotten the date when she told me she was pregnant. Perhaps something happened that evening which caused the number to stick in Sidney's mind and he recalled it when working out how to break into my computer. And he could judge why I would consider that number to be utterly safe and therefore might use it as my code.'

'You have a vivid imagination.'

Gregg hesitated, left.

Twenty-Five

S aturday was cloudless, the air was filter clear, and by
ten thirty the sun was warm enough to make people
briefly forget winter lay ahead.

'Today,' Wendy said, 'we are going out.'

'I'd rather stay here,' Gregg said dully.

'Which is why we are going to enjoy our delayed celebration.'

'Celebrate the mess I'm in?'

'When we became engaged.'

'That!'

'The day means so little to you?'

'Don't be ridiculous.'

'Am I being ridiculous? You sounded as if you'd rather
forget all about it.'

'It was the most wonderful day.'

'There's no need to bother to try to console me.'

'Can't you understand? Don't you realize what I'm going
through?'

'Of course I do.'

'No one will listen to the truth. I've become a pariah. An
accessory to the murder of a policeman. If someone from
the station saw me disappearing into quicksand, he'd laugh.'

'Make them understand how wrong they are. Fight back.'

'With two hands tied behind my back?'

'You've a tongue.'

'They're deaf to anything I say.'

'Then shout.'

'For God's sake, stop talking like a jolly hockey-sticks
counsellor.'

'Sorry,' she said bitterly.

'If you'd had any sense, you'd've refused me and then you wouldn't be married to someone who's going to end up in jail.'

'Stop it.'

'Unlike you, I'm facing facts.'

'Carry on doing that and you'll make me leave and stay with my sister.'

'You haven't got a sister.'

'I'll find one. For God's sake, Andy, snap out of it. Stop wallowing in disaster. All right, things don't look good at work, but count your blessings. We love each other, we're fit, and Junior is learning to play the drums.'

'But—'

'Keep telling yourself that however black things look, you're going to turn them white . . . Enough of all that. We buy a little smoked salmon, bread rolls, butter, ham, cheese, tomatoes, a bottle of wine, and one of those divine chocolate cakes en route. I'll pack things into the old cane basket your mother gave us and we'll drive to our romantic hideaway. What's more, we're going to have a paddle in the sea, whatever the temperature.'

'You're a bully.'

'Someone has to be,' she said, glad to note the change in his tone of voice.

They sat between two small dunes which had crowns of grass across the tops. They had eaten almost all the food and drunk three-quarters of the bottle of Châteauneuf-du-Pape. 'Do you remember—' She stopped.

'The fifth of November?'

'You must have cheered up since you're making inane comments.'

'Some wives laugh at their husbands' witticisms.'

'Maybe they have witty husbands. Kiss me.'

'You've always objected to anything more than a peck on the cheek in public.'

'I don't mind the seagulls watching.'

'When they're the souls of drowned sailors?'

'You're mixing them up with albatrosses.'

'Am I? I'm usually good at identifying birds.'

'When they have arms and legs. Now, will you please kiss me?'

Moments later, they lay back on the rug, enjoying the sunshine and the swish of advancing and receding small waves.

He spoke. 'I was incredibly lucky the day I met you at that dance.'

'It was at a cocktail party.'

'Of course. Molly Stevens gave it to greet the summer solstice or something.'

'It was Roger Appleby's party.'

'And he introduced us.'

'Jim Westry did.'

'A very precious young man.'

'A keep-fit fanatic with steel biceps.'

'I noticed you the moment I entered the room.'

'Your appreciation was all for the blonde with notable assets.'

'Nonsense!'

'Almost your first words to me, trying to impress me with your sophistication, were that it was as if the party were being held on Jura.'

'What was that supposed to mean?'

She laughed.

He suffered a sudden emotional chill. How long was left to him during which he could talk nonsense with her, see her day and night, enjoy the warmth of her character, the beauty of her smile? How long before he was locked up among men who would seize every chance to humiliate and hurt him because he had been a copper?

They were in the sitting room, facing the television. The programme was detailing the moulding of land by ice and water.

She broke a long silence. 'Are you watching?'

'Not really.'

She used the remote control to switch off the set. 'I want you to promise to do something for me.'

'If I can, I will.'

'Go to the station tomorrow morning and speak to Inspector Horton again.'

'What?'

'I know how difficult it will be for you after all that's happened, but ask him to give you the credit for all you've done since you've been in the force.'

'Because he, like everyone else, is convinced I sold information and therefore am partly responsible for Quale's death, he doesn't give a damn if I had a good record, now it's poisoned.'

'Try.'

'It would be useless.'

'For me and junior. You promised you would if you could. Please, please.'

'All right,' he finally muttered.

'Hold it,' the duty PC called out.

Gregg stopped, turned to face Catskill behind the front desk. 'It's OK, Mark, I need a word with the inspector.'

'Who doesn't want a word with you.'

'He owes it to me.'

'He owes the likes of you nothing. Get back to the gutters so as you can feel at home.'

'The quality of mercy is not strained, it's strangled.' He turned back towards the outer door.

'Jim, find something to fumigate the place,' Catskill called out.

At ten past nine that evening, she said, 'Will you have something to eat now?'

'I'm not hungry,' Gregg dully replied.

'But you must eat. Would you like eggs? Boiled, scrambled, an omelette?'

'Mark has had drinks, meals here. I've always thought

of him as a good friend, yet I've told you what he said as I left the station. Even if they can't prove what they're alleging, he won't have anything to do with me, any more than the others will.'

'You thought Andy was a friend.'

'He can't really be blamed for what's happened.'

'Are you crazy?'

'She's twisted his mind.'

'Only because he's so bloody weak.'

'Mark's no reason to turn on me unless he's ready to believe in my guilt solely because the others do. You expect a friend to stand by you in the face of rumours.'

'You may, but precious few do. It's become a world where only number one matters. Now, what are you going to have? Would you prefer cold meat left over from lunch because you didn't eat it or some chipolatas?'

'A boiled egg.'

'Two boiled eggs.' She left the room.

She had, he accepted, reason to be annoyed as well as sympathetic. He had become poor company. But when up to one's neck in quicksand and sinking, it was difficult to smile.

The front doorbell rang.

'I'll get it,' she called out.

It was late for a casual visitor, he mused, and no one had expressed a wish to visit them. He hoped Wendy would get rid of whoever it was. To have to find the effort to be politely welcoming was—

Wendy screamed.

He raced across to the door, flung it open. Just inside the front doorway was a man, face obscured by a multicoloured ski-mask; thickset, medium height, dressed in dark, nondescript clothing. He held a knife with a six-inch blade in his right hand. A vicious layabout, ready to steal anything which could be quickly sold. Then Gregg noticed how he held the knife loosely, the hilt in the palm of his hand, and that suggested he was an experienced knifeman, ready to flick the knife from one hand to the other in offence or defence.

He was not a casual thief. He came forward, his gaze fixed on Gregg. When level with Wendy, too shocked to have moved, he flicked the knife over to his left hand and used his right to slam her against the wall. She cried out as she collapsed to the floor.

Gregg stood still, balancing himself. Avoid the first attack and the advantage could be with him. The man moved with lithe speed for someone of his build. Two paces and he was within reach of Gregg, the knife flashed past Gregg's head, leaving a small, stinging cut. A misjudged attack? Or deliberately off target to feed the amusement of a sadistic killer?

Gregg had received no more training in self-defence than had any other policeman, but that had included how to obtain an arm lock guaranteed to immobilize an opponent. He aimed to apply it, was knocked off balance by a savage kick to his leg; as he regained his balance, a blow to the stomach filled it with fire and threw him to the ground. He tried to scrabble backwards, to gain the space to get to his feet and continue the unequal fight, but his hair was gripped, his head forced back, the blade of the knife came down towards his throat.

There was a crashing sound. Bits of pottery hit the ground around him. The man grunted, tried to rise, collapsed. Fighting the pain in his stomach, Gregg began to wriggle his way free of the other. Fingers gripped his shoulder; he bit down on them and forced them to release. He reached down to the man's crotch, squeezed and twisted with all his strength. The man bellowed, jerked himself free. Gregg got to his feet. The man was reaching for the knife. Gregg stamped down on the hand. Despite the injuries he had just suffered, again moving with unexpected speed, the man came to his feet, ran to the open front door, and out on to the street.

Gregg staggered to where Wendy stood, the shattered neck of Aunt Kit's ugly vase in her shaking hand. He put his arms around her.

As Horton came round the bonnet of the parked car, McGill stepped out on to the pavement. Together, they walked to

No. 15. Horton opened the gate and led the way up the mock flagstone path, rang the bell.

Wendy opened the door, stared at them with a surprise which quickly gave way to open dislike.

'Good morning, Mrs Gregg.' McGill spoke urbanely, smiled, apparently unaware of her obvious hostility.

'What do you want?'

'First, to say how very glad we are to learn you have suffered no lasting injury and your shoulder should soon be back to normal.'

'Is there anything else?'

'We should like to speak to your husband.'

'Can't you ever leave him alone?'

'We will not distress him.'

'No? What are you going to accuse him of this time? Injuring that swine of a man who attacked us?'

'My only comment is, what a pity your husband was unable to injure him far more severely. Mrs Gregg, as much as we regret having to be here, we must learn from him, and you, what happened last night.'

'Are you going to call him a liar once more?'

'No.'

She waited, they waited. Finally she said, 'If you're not going to go away, you'd better come in. Andy's in considerable pain, so please don't remain any longer than you have to.'

They followed her into the sitting room. Gregg sat on the settee, his back against an arm, his legs stretched out. He stared at them, uncertain, uneasy.

McGill said, 'The doctor has told me your injuries are responding well to treatment and you should before long be fit once more. I was very glad to learn that.' He turned to Wendy. 'Would you mind, Mrs Gregg, if we sat?'

'I'm sorry,' she replied, annoyed that his request had highlighted her deliberate lack of hospitality. 'Please do.'

They settled on two easy chairs. Wendy sat with Gregg, held his hand.

McGill spoke to Gregg. 'I hope you'll understand the

need to talk to you now; to learn from you exactly what happened.'

'Yes.'

'We'll be as brief as possible.'

Wendy suffered the need to ask, 'Would you like tea or coffee?'

'Thank you, no,' McGill answered. 'We had some coffee not long ago and you won't want us in the house for a moment longer than we have to be here.' He smiled.

She did not return the smile.

McGill asked Gregg, 'Will you describe events as far as you can remember them?'

Gregg did so, experiencing the illogical fear, which was haunting him, of what might have happened, but didn't.

'Did the man speak?'

'Not once.'

'Did you learn anything which might help identify him?'

'All I can say is that he's medium height, stocky, a very quick mover and an expert knifeman. The finger or fingers of his right hand must have been badly crushed when I stamped on them and may need hospital attention.'

'He gave no indication of why he intended to kill you?'

'He didn't have to.'

'Can you still not understand?' Wendy asked angrily.

'Yes, Mrs Gregg, but I need your husband to explain.'

'For God's sake, he was trying to kill Andy because—'

'OK, Wendy.' Gregg briefly gripped her hand tightly. 'He was trying to have me killed because I was getting too close to the truth about the sale of information, the way the money was laundered, the identities of those involved.'

'You have proof of that?'

'My attempted murder.'

Wendy refused to stay silent. 'And now I suppose you're going to say that's not enough. You still think it's all lies.'

'I believe your husband has spoken the truth. What I was asking him was if he could provide any hard proof. Considering the circumstances, it was extremely unlikely he could, but the question had to be asked. Let me assure you

I am convinced he was in no way involved in the sale of information. Further, I wish to apologize for having misjudged him and in self-defence can only say that the evidence had to be accepted at face value until it could be refuted.'

'If you had bothered to understand the kind of person he is, you wouldn't have made the mistake of believing him guilty.'

'I must agree.' He spoke to Gregg once more. 'You are, of course, to return to work, but not until you are declared a hundred per cent fit. In the meantime, I will make it clear to every member of the division that you were innocent of the sale of information and in no way did you play any part in the murder of PC Quale.'

Gregg wondered how his reinstatement would be received. With embarrassment because of memories? *Find something to fumigate the place.* Did he want to return to face people who had been so quick to think him a traitor?

McGill stood. 'Your are to be congratulated, Mrs Gregg, on having provided your husband with considerable support throughout and finally a very strong right arm.'

'I played lacrosse at school.'

He turned back to Gregg. 'If you do have the luck to remember anything more, let me or Inspector Horton know immediately.'

'What happens now?'

'The evidence will be re-examined to determine the future action which needs to be taken. This will, of course, include a request for the financial affairs of Lingwood to be very closely examined.'

They said goodbye, left. Wendy, who had accompanied them to the front door, returned. 'Was he saying Sidney will be arrested?'

'If sufficient proof is uncovered to convince the lawyers.'

She spoke with sudden passion. 'How could he? How could he have tried to have you murdered?'

'Someone once said that life is all about priorities. His priority is Gwen. Compared to his desire for her, nobody else, nothing else, is important.'

'If you again try to tell me that therefore he can't really be blamed, I'll throw something at you!'

'Since Aunt Kit only gave you the one vase, I don't feel too threatened.'

Pain awoke Gregg. He stared into the darkness which was only slightly lessened by street lighting. Cope. Why had he woken up for once remembering in part what he had been dreaming and known that Cope had been part of the dream? He had no friends or acquaintances of that name.

He went to turn over on to his other side, stopped. Moderate bruising, the doctor had said; bloody *im*moderate bruising would have been his description.

'Are you all right?' Wendy asked sleepily.

'Just a twinge.'

'Did you take two pain pills?'

'Yes.'

'Can I get you something? Heat can help. I'll switch the electric blanket on.'

'That'll fry us.'

'Then I'll get a hot water bottle.'

'Even hotter and the pain's gone.'

'I'll bet it hasn't. Men are so hopeless.'

Minutes passed. 'Howard Cope,' he said aloud.

'What's that?' she mumbled.

He didn't answer and soon her regular breathing told him she was once more asleep.

Release from the fears which had occupied his mind to the exclusion of all else had allowed him to recall and iden- tify those flappy ears. Several years back, he had arrested one man for theft and it had been clear another was also guilty, but there had been insufficient evidence to arrest him. In the greengrocer's in Myoe, that man had called himself Lingwood.

As the case had already proved, crimes involving several persons provided the risk that if one of them came under sharp suspicion, he would confess in order to gain a lesser sentence. Cope, judging the case was about to be broken wide open after he had been questioned, had probably left the greengrocer's and 'disappeared'. But now he was identified, he would be found, questioned, and would confess all he knew in an effort to escape the charge of murder.

Sidney had shown he placed no value on friendship. Yet Gregg could not escape the knowledge that when he provided Cope's name, he would be responsible for completing the wreckage of Sidney's life. Wendy would call him an utter fool for his instinctive reluctance to condemn Sidney to his fate. She would be right. But there were times when a man knew what he had to do and vainly wished he didn't.

He wondered how soon it would be before Gwen would find herself another man?